Hear

❧

Always There

Heartland

❧

Share every moment. . . .

Heartland

❧

Always There

by **Lauren Brooke**

SCHOLASTIC INC.

New York Toronto London Auckland Sydney
Mexico City New Delhi Hong Kong Buenos Aires

With special thanks to
Gill Harvey

No part of this publication may be reproduced in whole or in part, or stored in a retrieval system, or transmitted in any form or by any means, electronic, mechanical, photocopying, recording, or otherwise, without written permission of the publisher. For information regarding permission, write to Scholastic Inc., Attention: Permissions Department, 557 Broadway, New York, NY 10012.

ISBN 0-439-65368-1

Heartland series created by Working Partners Ltd., London.

Copyright © 2005 by Working Partners Ltd.
Published by Scholastic Inc. All rights reserved.

SCHOLASTIC and associated logos are trademarks and/or registered trademarks of Scholastic Inc. HEARTLAND is a trademark and/or registered trademark of Working Partners Ltd.

12 11 10 9 8 7 6 5 4 3 2 1   5 6 7 8 9 10/0
Printed in the U.S.A.   40
First printing, July 2005

To Kristin Earhart,
Amy's tireless and loving friend

Heartland

❧

Always There

Chapter One

❧

Amy stood under the scorching June sun and flicked the lunging whip so that the end snapped back against itself. "Trot on!" she ordered her young horse, Spindleberry.

The two-year-old bay snorted and broke into a trot, arching his neck and moving in neat, springy strides. Amy's boyfriend, Ty, jogged beside Spindle, his hand barely touching the lunging cavesson.

"Good boy, Spindle!" Amy encouraged. She watched the leggy bay trot briskly around the sand arena, his coat turning golden in the sunshine. Spindle was making good progress on the lunge, Amy mused, responding to her voice and keeping to a wide, even circle. Before long, he wouldn't need Ty running at his side.

"And . . . walk," Amy instructed after Spindle and Ty had finished another lap.

"Thanks," Ty said with a grin, slightly out of breath.

Amy smiled and flicked the whip again to keep Spindle's walk active. The pony responded willingly, stretching out his neck and lengthening his stride.

It was more than a year since Spindleberry had first come to Heartland, one of eight horses rescued from an overheated cattle truck. Three of the horses had not survived, and of the other five, Spindle was the only one still at Heartland. Amy had kept him as her own horse and was training him with the help of Ty and their stable hand, Joni, using the gentle Heartland methods Amy had learned from her late mother.

"Amy, phone for you!" Joni called, appearing at the gate. "It's Soraya."

"Be right there!" Amy said.

She reined Spindle to a halt and jogged over to Ty to hand him the line and whip. "I need to take this call," she said. "Just do two or three more circuits with him, OK?"

Ty nodded. "Sure. I'll get Joni to lead him," he said, beckoning to the stable hand. Amy thanked Ty, gave Spindle one more pat, and ran up the path to the farmhouse, wondering what Soraya was calling about. Again. She and Amy were about to wrap up their senior year of high school. Classes had already ended and graduation was tomorrow, followed by an evening party for the whole class. Soraya was practically dying with excitement over all the plans. But Amy was having trouble sharing her friend's enthusiasm.

Up until the past fall, Amy had always planned to continue her work at Heartland after graduation. But Amy's unexpectedly high SAT scores had led her to reconsider. After much thought, she had applied to the prestigious preveterinary program at Virginia Tech, a four-year university located about two hours from Heartland. When Amy finally told her family and friends that she had decided to apply to college, she was met with a tremendous outpouring of encouragement. Even Ty, who clearly had reservations about Amy's going away to school, had seemed genuinely excited for her. Then Amy received the acceptance letter from Virginia Tech in April, and everything suddenly became all too real. Ty was *still* supportive about her choice, but Amy sensed a growing distance between them — a feeling that he, like everyone else at Heartland, was mentally preparing himself for her departure. And Amy *was* anticipating the possibilities that college held, but she still hadn't made peace with the fact that she was leaving behind her beloved home and the work she had come to treasure — the work she had inherited from her mother.

"Hey, you took your time!" Soraya's voice greeted Amy when she picked up the receiver.

"I was down in the training ring," Amy explained.

"Listen," Soraya said urgently. "I just called the salon. They have an opening! We can have our hair done at the same time, first thing tomorrow."

"Oh," Amy said. "Actually, I wasn't planning on getting my hair done."

Soraya gave a heavy sigh. "Amy, this is *graduation.* You want to look good, don't you? Come on, you did it for Lou's wedding."

Amy laughed. "That's a surprise. Soraya's being persistent," she said. "What time is the appointment?"

"Eight sharp. Is that too early for you?"

"No way," Amy assured her. What with her hectic schedule at Heartland, Amy was used to rising at dawn.

"Oh, I am so psyched!" Soraya squealed. "So I'll see you first thing tomorrow?"

"I'll be there," Amy promised. She hung up, shaking her head, and walked into the kitchen.

Amy was surprised to find her sister, Lou, sitting at the table chatting with their grandfather's friend, Nancy.

"You're still here!" Amy exclaimed. Since her wedding that winter to Scott Trewin, the local vet, Lou had moved out of Heartland. Now she drove to the stable every day but usually left to be home in time for dinner with her husband.

Lou smiled. "Scott's been called away to see a horse. He's not sure how long it'll take, so I thought I'd stick around here for dinner. *And* I thought you might need some help getting ready for your big day tomorrow!"

"Don't remind me," Amy groaned. "Soraya just bullied me into having my hair done."

"I'm glad," Lou said approvingly. "She should also be there tomorrow to make sure that your dress isn't wrinkled or covered in straw."

Amy grinned in spite of herself. "I'm not a complete mess. I looked fine for your wedding, didn't I?" she protested. "But I'm so glad you're staying for dinner. What's this about Scott seeing a horse? Anyone we know?"

Lou shook her head. "I didn't get a chance to ask."

As Nancy and Lou began preparing dinner, Amy headed out into the yard. The shadows were lengthening, and she saw Ty leading Spindle up the track toward the stables.

"I'll start bringing the horses in," she called.

Ty raised his hand in acknowledgment. Amy collected a couple of halters and lead ropes from the tack room, then walked down to the pastures. Most of the horses were being kept outdoors for the summer months, but four were still being brought in for the night.

Amy let herself into the top pasture and walked slowly toward Moonstone, a gray Thoroughbred mare with a flaxen mane and tail. Moonstone's problem was that she started napping whenever her owner tried to ride her out. Amy had been working with the horse successfully for a few weeks now. The mare raised her head as Amy approached, blowing through her nose in welcome. Amy hid the halters behind her back and held out a handful of alfalfa cubes.

"Good girl," she murmured as Moonstone ambled forward. She let the mare lip the cubes from her palm and slipped a halter over her ears. Before leading her to the gate, Amy looked around the pasture, checking on the other horses. Most were grazing peacefully, but Sugarfoot, one of the permanent residents, caught her eye. The adorable Shetland had come to Heartland when his owner had died unexpectedly two years earlier.

The tiny pony had been lying down, but he started to heave himself up when he saw Moonstone eating the alfalfa cubes. Amy frowned. Was it her imagination, or was Sugarfoot having more trouble standing than usual?

The pony shook his mane and snorted, righting himself. He seemed fine, but Amy decided to look more closely at him all the same. She tied Moonstone to the gate and walked over to Sugarfoot, watching as he wobbled over to meet her.

"Here, boy," she called, offering him a few alfalfa cubes.

Sugarfoot stretched out his neck, his nostrils flaring greedily.

"I think I'm going to take you in for the night," Amy

said thoughtfully as the Shetland started to munch the treats.

She eased a halter over his ears and led him over to Moonstone. There was definitely something odd about Sugarfoot's stride, Amy noticed. It wasn't lameness exactly, or the heavy-heeled walk of a horse with laminitis. It was more that his hind legs seemed a little clumsy and stiff, especially on his left side. Amy mentally ran through a list of possible ailments, but she came up blank.

Amy led the pair up to the yard, Sugarfoot's little hooves crunching on the sandy path at double the rate of Moonstone's long, even strides. Joni was doing the rounds with hay nets and had already put one in Moonstone's stall. When Amy led Moonstone inside and unclipped her halter, the mare headed straight for the hay net and began pulling at it eagerly. Amy patted the mare and went back to where she had tied Sugarfoot by the tack room.

"Is Sugarfoot OK?" Joni asked Amy, glancing over.

"I'm not sure," Amy admitted. "His hind legs seem kind of wobbly, so I thought I'd bring him in, just in case there's something wrong."

"His walk *is* a little off," Joni agreed as Amy led the Shetland across the yard and unbolted his door. "Do you have any idea what it could be?"

"Not yet." Inside the stall, Amy unclipped Sugarfoot's halter and ran her hand down each of his legs in turn, while Joni leaned over the half door and watched. "There's no heat in his legs. I don't think it's any kind of regular lameness," Amy observed. She looked at the pony's eyes, gently pulling back the skin. "His mucous membranes look a bit pale. I'll give him some folic acid and see how he is in the morning. He might be anemic."

"Sounds wise," said Joni. She grinned. "You are such a budding vet! But is there anything I can do to help? Aren't you graduating tomorrow? You won't have time to check on him —"

"I'll make time," Amy said determinedly. She hadn't meant to cut Joni off, so she smiled apologetically. "But if you're doing the feeds, you could give him a dose of folic acid while you're at it. And if you ever feel like singing to him, he'll love you forever."

Joni raised an eyebrow and cocked her head. "Why's that?"

"Well, as you know, Sugarfoot was grieving for his owner, Mrs. Bell, when he came here," Amy said. Sugarfoot had been at Heartland much longer than Joni, but Amy had filled the stable girl in on the horse's backstory when Joni first joined the team. "Nothing we did seemed to reach him enough to pull him out of his sorrow. It was awful. We thought he was just going to fade away and die. But then Lou remembered that Mrs. Bell used to sing all the time. So Lou started singing to Sugarfoot — and he got better!"

"That's amazing," said Joni. "So that's why Lou's so attached to him."

Amy nodded, letting herself out of the stall. "He's definitely her favorite horse on the yard." She refrained from mentioning that Mrs. Bell had died shortly after Amy and Lou's mother, Marion, had passed away. Sugarfoot and Lou had seemed to go through the process of grieving together.

Amy headed down to the pasture to bring in the rest of the horses, leaving Joni to finish the evening feeds. She leaned on the pasture gate for a few minutes, watching the horses graze in the fading light. It seemed incredible that tomorrow would be her last day as a high school student. All that running around to get the chores done beforehand, all the scrambling to fit in her homework — over for good.

But although Amy was glad to be moving on from that hectic way of life, she was dreading what else the upcoming change would entail. There were just a few short months of summer left before she started at Virginia Tech.

Pushing the thought away, Amy opened the gate and caught the roan cob, Romany, then had to chase around after the aptly named chestnut gelding, Mischief. By the time Amy got back up to the yard, Lou was calling for her from the farmhouse, and Amy had to leave Ty and Joni to finish the chores.

"Soraya just called again," Lou said as Amy entered the kitchen. "She left a message. Something about the graduation party."

"That girl." Amy sighed.

Lou gave her a sympathetic smile. "I know you hate this kind of stuff," she said. "But we're all going to be so proud of you tomorrow. You *are* looking forward to it a little, aren't you?"

"Of course I am," Amy said, suddenly feeling awkward. She *was* proud to be graduating. But it just felt so final. After tomorrow, there was no looking back. College — and the future — loomed ahead.

Lou walked around the kitchen table and gave her sister a big hug. "I am, too. It's going to be a day to remember."

Amy returned Lou's embrace, then grabbed the cutlery to set the table as Grandpa came in from the yard. With Nancy stirring pasta sauce at the stove and Lou flipping through mail at the table, it felt just like old times. Amy smiled to herself, remembering the night before Lou's wedding. She had been worried that life would be so different when her sister moved out. In fact, things hadn't changed much at all.

As for the change *she* was about to make, Amy felt butterflies in her stomach just thinking about it. She reflected on the fact that once she went off to college, she wouldn't be able to come home for dinner.

❧

Amy slept badly that night. Lou had fussed over her all evening, smoothing out Amy's dress and making her try it on with different necklaces. The dress itself had been Lou's — worn to parties when she had lived in New York. It was a silk knee-length dress in deep aquamarine with cap sleeves. Grandpa and Nancy had raved over Amy in the dress, and Nancy had produced a pair of earrings and a choker that went perfectly with the blue fabric. Amy had found herself getting into the spirit of the evening as she twirled around, admiring her outfit in the mirror.

But now that she was lying alone in bed, Amy's thoughts were darker. The guilt and doubt that had nagged at her all day rushed to the forefront of her mind. Suddenly, she found herself remembering her mother. Marion had always encouraged Amy to study hard, but her mother's top priority had been Heartland. Would Marion have really approved of Amy choosing college over the stable? Amy tossed and turned, wishing for sleep. She couldn't look pale and haggard for graduation tomorrow.

Amy drifted off eventually but woke as dawn began to break. Her eyes stinging, she sat up and looked out the window, watching the gray light turn pink. Suddenly remembering that she had brought Sugarfoot in for the night, Amy swung her legs out of bed, dressed hurriedly, and went down to the yard. It was still very early. Ty and Joni hadn't arrived yet. Sugarfoot was dozing when Amy peered over his half door.

"Sugarfoot!" she called softly, sliding back the bolt.

Sugarfoot raised his head at the sound of her voice. He was standing with his legs slightly splayed. Watching his movements carefully, Amy entered the stall, looking for any signs of the clumsiness she had seen the night before. The Shetland lurched as he made room for her in the stall, and Amy frowned. She bent down and placed one hand on the pony's haunches, asking him to move sideways. He did as she asked, but there was a definite wobble in his hind legs — and as Amy had noticed the night before, the problem seemed worse on his left side.

Amy stroked the pony's neck, thinking. She had never seen symptoms like this before. Could it be some kind of virus? She didn't want to worry Lou, knowing how much Sugarfoot meant to her sister, but Amy realized that she was going to have to call Scott.

Amy quickly let herself out of Sugarfoot's stall and was heading back toward the house when Ty pulled into the driveway in his pickup.

"Hey, graduate!" he called. "Aren't you supposed to be getting ready?"

Amy smiled. "I have about an hour before I see Soraya," she said. Then her smile faded. "Actually, I came down to look at Sugarfoot. There's something wrong with him, Ty."

Ty instantly looked concerned. "What's the matter?"

"There's some kind of weakness in his hind legs. I noticed it last night," Amy explained. "Come and look, OK? I was about to call Scott. I'm really worried."

Amy and Ty hurried to Sugarfoot's stall. He was still standing with his legs splayed, as though he couldn't quite balance properly. Amy got the Shetland to step sideways, showing Ty the pony's strange loss of coordination in his hind legs. His flanks were damp with sweat, too.

"What do you think it is?" Amy asked.

Ty shook his head. "I've never seen anything like it. You're right. We should call Scott. But I know you have a lot to do this morning, Amy. Why don't I give him a call?"

Amy shook her head. "Soraya — and the hair salon — can wait. I'll call Scott right now. Can you just keep an eye on Sugarfoot?"

Ty agreed, and Amy went inside. She dialed Lou and Scott's home number and, to her dismay, it was her sister who answered. Lou's voice was froggy with sleep.

"Amy, what time is it?" she mumbled.

"Around seven," Amy replied. "I'm sorry I woke you, Lou, but is Scott there?"

"Why?" Lou's voice became alert at once. "Is everything OK?"

Amy took a deep breath. "It's Sugarfoot," she said. She explained the problem.

"What do you mean, he seems wobbly? Why didn't you tell me last night?" Lou demanded, all in one breath.

"It's probably nothing serious," Amy told her. "But I thought Scott should have a look."

"OK," Lou said, sounding calmer. "Scott's over at the clinic now, but I'll tell him to go over once he's back. I'll be over in half an hour. Oh, and, Amy, what were you doing out on the yard this morning? Aren't you —"

"I know." Amy cut her off. "I'm going to take a shower now. When I see you next, I'll be in cap and gown!"

∾

An hour later, Amy breathlessly arrived at the hair salon, wearing the silk aquamarine dress and holding her graduation gown and mortarboard in a garment bag. Soraya's parents would be driving them straight to the high school after the appointment, which meant Amy wouldn't have a chance to go back to Heartland and check on Sugarfoot.

Just as Amy had been getting into Grandpa's car to make the eight o'clock appointment, Scott had pulled into the Heartland driveway. Amy had wanted to stay while Scott examined the Shetland, but Scott urged Amy along, assuring her that he would call her cell phone if there were problems. Amy anxiously checked her phone as she slid into the black swivel chair beside Soraya.

"What's wrong?" Soraya asked. Her curly black hair was being pinned back by her hairdresser, and her dark eyes were dancing with excitement.

Amy explained about Sugarfoot as a hairdresser appeared behind her and began spraying her hair with a mist of water to dampen it. Soraya listened sympathetically, then said, "Well, if Scott's on the case, I'm sure it will all be fine, Amy. Don't let it ruin your day."

"I won't," Amy said, but she realized she didn't sound very convincing. The hairdresser was carefully rolling up her straight light-brown hair in a French twist.

"You'll forget all your worries at the party tonight," Soraya assured her, giving Amy a big smile in the mirror. "It's going to be so much fun. Actually, I called yesterday to talk about that. Did Lou give you the message? I wanted to know if you were bringing Ty or not."

Amy shot a confused look at Soraya, disrupting the hairdresser's work. "Why wouldn't I bring Ty?" Amy asked, a note of defensiveness in her voice. She had been looking forward to Ty taking her to the graduation party, which would be held at the class president's house. Ty had been Amy's date to her prom back in May; Amy remembered how wonderful it had been, whirling around with him on the school gymnasium's dance floor, under the streamers and fairy lights. Girls in her grade who'd never seen Ty before whispered admiringly about the very cute and mysterious older boy who held Amy in his arms, and Amy had felt pleased and proud.

"Well," Soraya replied hesitantly, "it's just that I know sometimes it's been awkward, in the past, with Ty not having graduated from high school and all. And everyone at the party will have just graduated, and we'll all be jabbering away about college and stuff. . . ." Soraya trailed off, shrugging apologetically.

Amy studied her reflection as her friend's words sunk in. It was true. Ty had dropped out of high school in order to commit full-time to Heartland, and Amy sometimes did sense a distance between him and her high school friends — as if he couldn't entirely relate to their experiences. Amy couldn't imagine not having Ty with her at the party, but she could also see him feeling left out, especially if everyone's conversation centered around graduation and college plans.

"It doesn't matter," Amy told Soraya confidently as the hairdresser patted her French twist into place and doused it with hair spray. "Ty won't feel awkward at all.

He's been so understanding about my going away to Virginia Tech."

But as Amy studied her newly sophisticated self in the mirror, she felt a pang of uncertainty. She realized that if people would be talking about college at the party, that would only highlight the fact that Amy would be leaving Heartland — and Ty — at the end of the summer.

℞

The school grounds had been transformed for the graduation ceremony. Rows of chairs were laid out in front of a big open-air stage, and when Amy and Soraya arrived before ten, the seats started filling up with the friends and family of the senior class. Soraya, Amy, and their friend Matt, wearing their caps and gowns, marched down the aisle in time to "Pomp and Circumstance," then took their places in the first few rows. They turned around constantly, craning their necks to see if their families had arrived yet. Soraya spotted her parents and waved frantically. Matt's were not far behind, and they gave Amy a special smile, but there was no sign of anyone from Heartland.

Amy began to worry. In a flash, she thought of Sugarfoot. Maybe something had happened to the pony. But why hadn't Scott called? She sat with her hands in her lap, nervously biting her lower lip as the school band started playing and the principal stepped up to the podium.

Soraya squeezed her arm sympathetically. "They'll be here," she whispered.

Amy smiled weakly. She cast a glance over her shoulder once more but couldn't spot any of her relatives. The principal finished his introductory speech to a big round of applause and then began calling students to the stage in alphabetical order.

Ashford, Bellini, Butler, Davies, De Silva, Drayton . . . Amy's heart began to thud as the names approached Fleming. Even though she'd had mixed feelings about this day, she still wanted more than anything to share it with her family and Ty.

"Amy Fleming," called the principal.

Amy stood up, her knees trembling, and made her way to the stage. As she climbed the steps, she glanced over her shoulder one last time. Relief flooded through her as she saw Lou, Scott, and Ty hurriedly slipping into an empty row of seats, with Grandpa and Nancy just behind. Lou waved, and Amy grinned nervously. Then she met Ty's gaze and held it for a heartbeat.

Amy walked across the stage, accepted her diploma, and shook the principal's hand. As she stepped off the stage, she looked back at Ty. He was clapping along with everyone else, but there was an unmistakable sadness in his green eyes.

And in that moment, as Amy numbly switched the tassel on her cap from one side to the other, she decided that she couldn't put Ty through the graduation party tonight. And she wasn't going, either. For the rest of the summer, she wanted to spend all her free time with Ty — and at Heartland. That might not make the eventual separation any easier, but Amy couldn't bear to have it any other way.

Chapter Two

After the ceremony, Amy gathered with her family in the parking lot, along with the crush of other graduates.

Jack immediately wrapped Amy in a big hug. "I'm very proud of you," he whispered into her ear. "And your mom would have been, too."

At the mention of Marion, Amy felt her heart swell. "Thanks, Grandpa," she whispered back. Suddenly, her worries came spilling out to him. "I just hope I'm doing the right thing," she added. "You know, going away to college?"

"Of course you are," Grandpa assured her. He pulled away and put his hands on her shoulders. Amy saw that there were tears in his eyes, and she felt her throat tighten.

"But do you think Mom would have thought so, too?" she asked, searching his face.

Grandpa smiled, the crow's-feet around his eyes creasing. "Marion gave you your gift with horses, Amy," he said. "She would want you to make the very best use of it, and she would have backed you every step of the way. You know, there were so many times when she wished she'd had a vet's training. So don't you doubt yourself for a moment."

Amy nodded as Grandpa squeezed her hands in his. Then as Nancy stepped forward, Amy smiled.

"Congratulations, dear," said Nancy, kissing her.

Amy hugged the older woman and turned to Ty. He put his arm around her shoulder, and Amy leaned into his familiar warmth.

"You looked fantastic up there," Ty said, gazing down at her. He paused and swallowed hard. "In another world."

Amy shook her head. "I'm still firmly in *this* world," she said. "Speaking of which, how's Sugarfoot? Did something happen? Is that why you guys were late?"

Scott shook his head. "I examined Sugarfoot this morning. To be honest, I'm not sure what's wrong with him, so I'm going to come back to do some tests tomorrow."

"And it's *my* fault we were late," Lou chimed in, coming forward to wrap Amy in a hug. "I'm so sorry. I misplaced my purse at the last minute. You must have been so worried we wouldn't get here in time! But there was something important in my purse that I wanted to bring." She grinned and handed Amy an envelope.

"It's OK," Amy said. "You got here in the end." Curious, she looked down at the envelope.

"Go on, open it!" Lou urged her.

Amy opened the envelope. Inside was a beautiful handmade card. Out of it slipped a check for an amount of money that made Amy gasp.

"Our dear Amy," the card read. "Congratulations on your graduation. We wish we could be there to share your day with you. All our love and best wishes for your exciting future. Dad, Helena, and Lily."

Amy looked up. "Oh, Lou!" she exclaimed. "It's from Dad! And I'll be able to put this money toward school books or new clothes."

Lou nodded, her face glowing with happiness. "You can call to thank him later today," she suggested in a maternal tone."

"Congrats," Scott said, kissing Amy's cheek. "Look at you — the budding vet!"

"Not yet," Amy said bashfully.

"Yeah, give her a rest, Scott," Lou teased. "Let her be just a regular seventeen-year-old for today. After all, Amy, don't we have your big graduation party tonight?"

Amy shook her head, turning to Ty and taking his

hand. "I've decided not to go to the party," she told her family simply. "I'm sure it will be fun and all, and I'll miss my classmates, but . . ." She squeezed Ty's hand. "There's no place I'd rather be tonight than at Heartland, with all of you."

Amy had already told Soraya of her decision to skip the party, and her best friend had been upset — but she'd understood. She and Amy had made a date to see each other later in the week.

Lou smiled and touched Amy's arm. "If that's what you really want to do, then I'm so happy. Nancy and I are going to have a busy afternoon. We're going to make this one unforgettable Heartland celebration!"

&

Lou was as good as her word. While she, Nancy, Grandpa, and Scott drove to the store to buy the makings of a special meal, Amy joined Ty in his pickup for the drive back to Heartland.

As soon as she got home and changed out of her cap and gown, Amy went straight to Sugarfoot's stall, with Ty on her heels. The pony pricked his ears and whickered a greeting when they looked over the half door, and Amy smiled. He seemed in good spirits, and his hind legs were no more wobbly than they'd been that morning. Maybe the pony was all right after all.

"Let's go down to the pastures," Amy said, twining her

fingers through Ty's. "I'd like to see Sundance and Spindle."

Ty nodded and they walked down past the barn. The horses in the pasture were bathed in warm afternoon sunlight, and Amy breathed in the pollen-scented air with a deep feeling of contentment. Sundance wandered over to the gate, soon joined by Spindle and some of the others, ever hopeful for horse cookies.

Amy frowned as she looked down at Lou's silky dress. "No treats in my pockets, I'm afraid," she confessed, stroking Spindle's soft nose. "Maybe I should've changed into jeans," she told Ty with a small laugh.

"Let's go inside," Ty suggested. "It's been a long morning."

Amy realized how drained she felt, too. Graduation had certainly been emotional, in every way. She sighed happily as Ty slipped his arm around her waist and they walked back to the house, relieved she was staying home for the night.

Nancy was unloading groceries from her car in the driveway, and Amy and Ty hurried over to help her. Soon, everyone was pitching in with the preparations. Grandpa put on music and decorated the kitchen with balloons and streamers while the others tended to the food. Scott scrubbed potatoes, Ty chopped vegetables, Amy and Joni collected fresh herbs from the garden, and Lou and Nancy busied themselves with the chicken.

When night fell they gathered around the table, which was lit by candlelight and laden with a big roast chicken, potatoes, and fresh salad. Amy felt a blaze of happiness. She looked across the table at Ty and smiled. Who needed a silly old graduation party? This was where she belonged.

❧

"Hey! Stop that!" Joni called across the yard the next morning as Amy was mucking out the stalls. Amy looked at Joni in surprise, stopping her work.

"It's the first day of your summer vacation," Joni explained, jogging over and taking the fork away from Amy. "You should be relaxing and basking in your graduation glory."

"When have you known me to relax?" Amy teased.

"Well, Ty's doing the feeds, and he challenged me to muck out in record time. You wouldn't want to stop me, would you?" Joni grinned.

Amy laughed. "I have to do *something* around here," she said. "It's not like I'm gone yet!" Her tone was light, but she felt a pang as she spoke those words.

"Sundance was looking a little restless out in the pasture this morning. Do you think a trail ride would do him good?"

Amy nodded. "Me and him both, actually. Thanks, Joni."

She brought Sundance to the yard and tacked him up. He butted her playfully and Amy teasingly admonished him.

She swung herself into the saddle and adjusted the stirrups. Her feet hung below Sundance's belly. Spindle would be ready to ride soon and he'd be better suited to Amy, since he was a whole hand taller than Sundance.

When the buckskin pony realized that they were heading out onto the trails, he began to prance and snort in excitement, and Amy smiled. He was such a character. *I'll miss him,* she thought.

"Have fun!" Joni called as Amy clattered out of the yard. Amy waved to her, grateful that the thoughtful stable hand had made her take a break from the chores.

Sundance calmed down once they were climbing the ridge, and he trotted steadily up the track. Amy let herself relax into his familiar rhythm, remembering the times she had competed him at shows. He'd been an enthusiastic little jumper, always willing to put in a huge effort. Amy had such a history with this special horse.

The track opened out into a field, and Amy pushed Sundance into a canter, steering him with her legs toward the fallen logs that lay across the grass. Sundance cleared them with an exuberant kick of his heels, and Amy laughed out loud. When it was time to go back home, Sundance's trot slowed. His ears flicked to and fro as Amy hummed a tune to herself. Amy felt relaxed and mellow. Her anxieties about her future seemed to have evaporated and she let herself savor the peaceful, precious moment.

🐛

Back on the yard, Lou was coming out of Sugarfoot's stall. She looked concerned, and Amy dismounted hurriedly.

"Is Sugarfoot OK?" she asked Lou as she ran up the stirrup leathers. "He looked the same when I saw him this morning."

Lou stopped and walked over to Amy. "There's no change," she said. "But he seemed to be sweating a bit more than usual. Scott's got a whole herd of cattle to inoculate today, so he can't come over to do the tests until this evening."

"The more I think about it, the more it looks like some kind of vitamin deficiency that's affecting his muscles," Amy commented thoughtfully.

Lou nodded. "I guess it could be that." She ran a hand through her blond hair. "Oh, and I meant to tell you. We're getting a new arrival tomorrow afternoon. It's the horse that Scott went to see on Thursday."

"Great," said Amy. "What's his story?"

"The owner fell while jumping at a show and broke her arm," said Lou. "Fanfare — that's the horse — needs to rebuild his confidence while she recovers."

Amy thought that Lou looked very uncomfortable as she spoke. She didn't meet Amy's gaze, and her face seemed pale. *She must be really worried about Sugarfoot,* Amy thought. Her sister felt very close to the pony.

Lou went back into the house, so Amy finished untacking Sundance and gave him a quick rubdown before taking him back to the pasture. Ty had been clearing away the droppings and met her at the gate with a wheelbarrow.

"Good ride?" he asked with a grin. "Joni and I decided you deserved a break."

"You guys . . ." Amy said, unclipping the pony's halter. Sundance snorted and trotted off, his tail held high. "It was wonderful. But listen, Ty. Lou just told me there'll be a new horse arriving tomorrow. His name's Fanfare. Apparently he needs to regain confidence after a fall."

"Shouldn't be a problem," said Ty. "Do you think he'll be kept in?"

"Not sure," said Amy. "Lou didn't give me all the details. We'll have to ask her before he arrives tomorrow."

"OK. I'll just empty this, and I'll be in for breakfast," Ty said as they walked up the track.

Breakfast wasn't usually a big deal on Saturdays, but in honor of Amy's graduation Grandpa had made waffles. The delicious smell welcomed her as she walked into the kitchen and she breathed in deeply.

"They look fantastic, Grandpa," Amy said as he put a plateful of waffles on the table. "I can't believe that I'm starving after the amount I ate last night!"

"Plenty more where those came from!" said Grandpa. "Dig in before they get cold."

Amy put two waffles on her plate as Lou appeared from the office and sat down. Ty and Joni came in together and took off their yard boots before joining them at the table.

"Coffee, anyone?" asked Jack.

"Mmm, please, Grandpa," said Amy. She turned to her sister. "Lou, is Fanfare going to be stabled, or can we keep him out?"

Lou looked up sharply. "Fanfare?"

"Yeah — the horse arriving tomorrow?" Amy reminded her gently. "Ty and I were just wondering about him. Is he a competition horse?"

Lou poured some maple syrup over her waffle and shrugged. "No, but I think we'll need to bring him in at night."

Amy frowned. It wasn't like her sister to be so vague. Lou looked preoccupied, and Amy guessed she was still thinking about Sugarfoot. The sooner Scott came over to do those tests, the better.

When two servings of Grandpa's waffles had been polished off by the group around the table, Amy collected everyone's plates and took them to the sink. "Thanks, Grandpa," she said, pulling on her boots. "I feel like everyone's been spoiling me!"

Through the open door she saw a vehicle coming up the driveway and recognized the feed delivery truck. "I'll take care of this," she called to the others as the truck came to a halt. The driver jumped out, his delivery sheet ready.

"Heartland?" he asked as Amy came forward to meet him. "Four bags of meadow mix, one each of pony nuts, oats, and chaff."

"Hmm. That doesn't sound right," Amy said. "We don't usually get that much meadow mix. Can I see the list?"

"That's what it says," the driver said matter-of-factly. "Not much I can do about it." He handed his sheet to Amy and went to the back of the truck to unload.

Amy looked at the sheet. The driver was right; the list was clear enough. She thought quickly. With most of the horses out, and those that were inside on similar feeds, more meadow mix wasn't such a bad idea. It was cheaper than oats, too. Still puzzled, Amy signed for the delivery and helped the driver carry the bags to the feed room.

The van had pulled away and Amy was refilling the feed bins when Joni popped her head in the door. "Everything OK?" she asked.

"Well . . . something's a little weird," Amy admitted. "The order seems to have changed."

"Oh, you mean the extra meadow mix?" Joni asked, coming into the feed room. "I made that change. It seemed more affordable."

Amy looked up at her in surprise. Joni was right, but since when did she make decisions about the feed order? Amy's face must have betrayed her emotion.

"I did check with Lou," Joni added in a slightly apologetic tone.

Amy forced a smile. "Well, in that case . . ." She laughed awkwardly. "I just wish someone had told *me*, that's all."

Joni bit her lip. "I'm sorry, Amy," she said. "It's no big deal, is it?"

Amy shook her head. "It's fine," she said. She watched as Joni headed back outside and felt a lump rise up in her throat. *Why should I get so upset about meadow mix?* Amy wondered. But then she realized that her exchange with Joni was about something much bigger: her sense that everyone was almost behaving as if she'd already left.

❧

After lunch, Amy brought Spindleberry in from the pasture and groomed him thoroughly on the front yard. He was doing well with his early training, but he wouldn't be strong enough for backing for another year. At least she'd be able to do the backing herself, next summer. In the meantime, Amy wanted to give him all the training she could.

She reached for a hoof pick and ran her hand down Spindle's near foreleg. He lifted his foot obligingly, then leaned against her as she deftly cleaned out his frog with the pick.

But the two-year-old was heavy, and Amy's knees began to buckle. "Hey!" she said, laughing. She put his hoof down and moved to the other foreleg. Instantly, Spindle leaned into her again, trusting her to support him completely.

"Spindle!" Amy exclaimed, pushing him away again. "I can't pick your hooves if you do that."

She managed to clean out the second hoof and straightened up, feeling secretly pleased. Spindle trusted her so much. He was certain that she could hold his weight.

Suddenly, Amy imagined how it would feel to have Spindle follow her around the ring in join up, the greatest expression of a horse's trust. But was Spindle ready for join up yet? Would he be able to cope with the early, painful part — the part in which she drove him away?

Looking at Spindle's calm, inquisitive expression, Amy knew that he *was* ready. And there was no time like the present. She felt a sudden rush. She was going to join up with Spindleberry as soon as she finished his hooves.

"I'm going to take Mischief out on the trails," said Ty,

walking past as Amy picked up a hind leg. "And I asked Joni to ride Moonstone. You don't need any help with Spindle this afternoon, do you?"

Amy straightened and shook her head. "No, that's fine." She smiled as Joni emerged from the tack room carrying Moonstone's tack. "In fact, I'm thinking of trying join up with Spindle."

"Join up?" Ty looked doubtful. "D'you think he's ready for that?"

"Actually, I do," said Amy. "He's grown so much recently."

"My mom usually waits till they're a little older before doing join up," Joni said tentatively.

Amy bristled. She almost felt as if Ty and Joni were ganging up on her. They were acting as if she *didn't* have Spindle's best interests at heart! She laid her hand on Spindle's neck. "I think he's ready," she insisted. "He trusts me totally. It can only be a good experience for him at this stage."

"Well . . . it could also go wrong," Ty pointed out.

Amy stared at him. "But join up is the most natural thing a horse can do," she reminded him. "It's all about choosing to be with the herd rather than being shut out from it. In the wild, horses learn that almost as soon as they're born. They have to."

"That's true," Ty admitted, looking a little sheepish.

"I hadn't looked at it like that," Joni agreed. She

hesitated, then smiled at Amy. "I guess you're right. I hope it goes well."

Amy nodded, still feeling a bit huffy. But she didn't want to seem ungracious, so she smiled. "Have a good ride, guys. It was really gorgeous up on the ridge this morning."

Once Ty and Joni had ridden out of the yard, Amy led Spindle down to the training ring. She still felt unsettled that Ty and Joni had disagreed with her on the join-up issue. And it wasn't like Ty to question her judgment in front of someone else. Maybe he was already getting used to the idea of working just with Joni. Amy shook her head. She couldn't let these worries plague her now.

Amy unclipped Spindle's lead rope in the middle of the arena and shooed him away from her. Spindle backed off a couple of paces, then stood still, staring at her in bewilderment. It was a common reaction in horses that trusted her already, and Amy suppressed a smile. She drew herself up tall and ran toward Spindle purposefully. Spindle flinched and shied away, then started trotting around the outside of the ring, still looking unsettled by Amy's shift in behavior. Amy kept up his momentum by chasing after him with the loosely coiled rope, and after a couple of minutes he broke into a canter, the whites of his eyes showing his confusion.

Amy walked a smaller circle in the center of the ring

and kept the colt cantering around her. Every time Spindle slowed down she drove him on, refusing to let him rest. It was a good opportunity to watch his fluid, balanced movements — he was filling out well and growing into a fine, athletic horse, very different from the frightened youngster that had arrived in that horrible cattle truck more than a year before. Amy's stomach tightened at the thought of leaving Spindle behind to continue his training without her. She knew he would be in good hands, but it wasn't the same as training him herself.

Spindle clearly wasn't enjoying being in the lonely place on the outside of the ring. After a couple more circuits, he lowered his neck and began to make chewing motions with his lips. This was his manner of asking Amy to let him rejoin her. Amy wasn't surprised that the transition had happened so quickly. The two-year-old had no reason to want to avoid her — she was already an important member of his "herd," and he wanted to restore the bond between them. Amy let her shoulders drop, abandoning her aggressive stance, and slowly turned her back. Now was the moment that Spindle could choose to demonstrate his absolute trust in Amy by coming over to join her. Even though Amy was confident of what would happen, she still felt her heart beat faster as she waited.

Almost at once, Amy heard Spindle's footfalls heading across the school toward her. Happiness flooded her as she felt the horse's soft breath on her shoulder. Spindle blew gently into her ear, and she turned around.

"Oh, Spindle," she whispered, putting her arms around his neck. "You did it! I *knew* you were ready. And I'm so glad we joined up before I have to go."

Chapter Three

As Amy led Spindleberry back to the yard, she saw a shiny red car pull into the driveway. The door opened and Soraya stepped out, waving.

"Hey, Amy!" she called, her face glowing with excitement. Her black hair was in a high ponytail, and she looked radiant. "How do you like my graduation present?"

Amy tied up Spindleberry outside the tack room. "It's yours?" she asked incredulously, pointing to the gleaming car.

Soraya nodded. "Mom and Dad bought it for me. Isn't it beautiful? I couldn't *believe* it when they gave it to me this morning. I've been driving everywhere all day!"

Amy laughed. She would rather have Spindle than a car any day, but Soraya's joy was infectious. She grinned and obliged Soraya's order that she get inside and admire the spotless cream-and-red interior.

"So how was the party? Did I miss much?" Amy asked when she was allowed out of the car. "I'm just going to give Spindle a wipe down before I turn him out. You can come with me and tell me all about it."

"I wish you'd been there," Soraya said with a sigh. "I still can't believe you skipped it."

She reached out to hold Spindle as Amy gave him a quick once-over with a body brush. Then, as they led the colt down to the pasture, Soraya launched into a long, detailed description of the event, cataloging what everyone had worn, who had arrived with whom, and who had gone home early. Amy listened, amused, still feeling certain she'd done the right thing. It seemed as if talk at the party had centered on college. It would have been difficult for Ty to enjoy himself, and that meant that Amy wouldn't have really enjoyed it, either.

Amy gave Spindleberry's neck a final pat as they opened the gate, then unclipped his lead rope. "I'm glad you had such a great time," she told her best friend truthfully as the two-year-old cantered off. "But it was really nice to come back here instead. I know it seems strange, but . . . it was just where I wanted to be."

Soraya gave Amy a quick hug. "It's OK. I know I was sort of hyper about it all. But I completely understood. Actually, I have another plan."

"*Another* one?" Amy teased. "Uh-oh."

"Oh, come on! I asked Mom if I can throw a party myself, later on in the summer. I thought about what you said — you know, Ty not fitting in at the graduation party. It did make sense, but I don't want you guys to miss out. I thought I'd have something smaller, but one that different people can come to. Like Lou and Scott, Ben and Daniel if they want, Joni . . ."

Amy felt touched and also excited. It would be nice to celebrate with everyone before she left. "That's a fantastic idea."

"Do you think so?" Soraya looked delighted. "You'll definitely come?"

"I wouldn't miss it for the world," said Amy.

♋

When Soraya's car had disappeared down the driveway in a cloud of dust, Amy went to Sugarfoot's stall to see how the little Shetland was doing. Scott would be arriving soon to take the tests. As Amy moved around the pony, studying him, she noticed that he seemed to have lost weight. She stepped back, wondering if she was imagining it. She smiled to herself. His little belly was as round as ever! But then, as her gaze followed the line of his back, the truth hit her. Sugarfoot hadn't lost any fat — it was the muscles of his haunches that looked thinner. Muscle wastage. Loss of control in the hind legs. Amy's stomach dropped as the full meaning registered. Could the pony have some kind of degenerative disease?

She was running her hands along the pony's spine and haunches when she heard a pickup arrive in the yard. A couple of minutes later, Scott's head appeared over the half door.

"Hi, there," he greeted her. "Enjoying your first day of freedom?"

Amy smiled and nodded. "So far so good," she said. Her smile faded as she glanced down at Sugarfoot. "This little fella's not doing so well, though. Scott, I think he's losing muscle. Look."

"I'm sorry you've had to wait for me," said Scott apologetically. "I didn't have the right equipment to take a sample of spinal fluid yesterday."

Amy's mouth went dry. "Spinal fluid?"

"Don't panic. It's not as bad as it sounds," Scott reassured her. "If he has what I think he has, we should be able to treat him. I'll just get the stuff out of the car and let Lou know I'm here. I'll be with you in a second."

Amy's heart was still in her mouth as she stroked the Shetland's nose. She knew that if Scott had to take spinal fluid it meant something was wrong with the horse's central nervous system. But then she reminded herself that Scott had mentioned treatment, and she forced herself to calm down.

Scott soon reappeared with Lou, and Amy stood to one side as Lou rushed to kneel at the pony's head, her blue eyes dark with worry.

"He might not like this," Scott said as he took a long cerebrospinal syringe out of his bag. "I'll need you two to keep him calm."

Amy stroked Sugarfoot's mane while Lou cradled his head and fished some pony nuts out of her pocket. "Here you go," Lou murmured tenderly, then looked up anxiously at Scott as he prepared the syringe. "So what do you think it is?" she asked.

Scott looked down at his wife and smiled. "Don't worry, sweetheart," he said, and Amy felt a flood of relief at his comforting tone. "I think it might be something called equine protozoal myeloencephalitis. EPM for short. It's quite common."

"Common?" exclaimed Amy. "I've never heard of it."

"It's something that's only recently been understood, in the last ten years or so," said Scott. "The good news is that it's treatable as long as it's caught early enough. Quite an interesting disease. It's caused by a little protozoan, hence the name."

Amy wrinkled her forehead, thinking back to her high school biology class. "Like an amoeba?" she asked. "Aren't amoebas a kind of protozoan?"

"That's right," said Scott. "A tiny organism, basically." Scott positioned himself over the Shetland's back, carefully preparing the needle. Sugarfoot tensed as the long needle went in, and Lou stroked his forelock.

"Is it contagious?" Amy asked, not taking her eyes off the pony's gentle, trusting face.

"Not as such. The original carrier is the opossum, which passes it along the food chain," Scott explained. "Horses pick it up in grazing. If Sugarfoot is infected — and we can't be sure yet — we'll have to check the other residents because they obviously share the same pastures. We're not sure how long the disease can incubate, so he might have been carrying it for years, poor little guy."

Amy's heart turned a somersault at the idea of all the Heartland residents being at risk. She remembered the horrible trauma of the equine flu that had ravaged Heartland the year before. "Is it possible to treat it before symptoms appear?" she asked.

Scott nodded. "Yes. So there's no problem there. We just have to hope that we've caught Sugarfoot's problem in time — if it is EPM, of course."

Amy thought quickly. "But if he's had it for years, could we be too late?" she asked worriedly.

Scott shook his head. "Some horses carry it without ever developing symptoms, and it doesn't do them any harm. It's once the symptoms appear that you have to worry — but they can be reversed if they haven't progressed too far."

"And what *is* the treatment?" Lou's face was still tight with anxiety.

"An antiprotozoan drug," said Scott. He smiled at her. "They're pretty effective. And possibly some anti-inflammatory drugs once he's started to respond. I'd give him a good chance of pulling through. I don't want either of you worrying, OK?"

Amy and Lou exchanged relieved glances, and Lou gave the Shetland a hug. Amy watched him nosing at her sister's pockets for more treats, and she felt hopeful. Sugarfoot's symptoms were still mild, and she was sure she would have noticed if they had developed sooner.

As Scott packed away the sample and the syringe, Amy remembered something else she'd wanted to ask him. "So what's the story with the horse you saw on Thursday?" she queried. "You know, Fanfare? I'm looking forward to seeing him. Was he injured at all in the fall?"

Scott seemed preoccupied with his syringe case and glanced sideways at Lou, who frowned.

"Not physically," Lou answered. "The rider was, though, which is why Fanfare's lost confidence."

Scott gazed at Lou for a moment, then nodded. "The rider broke her arm," he agreed.

He continued to stare at Lou, who was looking back at her husband with a strangely determined expression. Amy felt uncomfortable. Why were they suddenly being cold with each other? Did it have something to do with Fanfare?

"I need to get back to the office," said Lou, giving Sugarfoot a last hug. "Can you come with me, honey? I need to go through your latest invoice."

Scott followed Lou onto the yard, leaving Amy in the Shetland's stall, feeling baffled. She stroked his mane, wondering why Lou and Scott had seemed so tense a moment before. They were usually very warm and affectionate toward each other. A shadow fell across the half door and Amy looked up. It was Ty.

"Everything OK?" he asked, his green eyes concerned. "Did Scott give a diagnosis?"

Amy nodded. "Sort of, but we can't be sure until the test results come back. He thinks it's equine protozoan . . . myelo something," she said. "EPM for short. Have you heard of it?"

"Doesn't ring any bells," said Ty. "Is it treatable?"

"Yes, thankfully — if we caught it in time." Amy frowned, still pondering her sister's behavior. "Lou and Scott were acting kind of weird, though."

"Weird?" Ty echoed, also frowning.

"Yeah. Everything went fine with Sugarfoot. But then Lou seemed to get really aloof with Scott." Amy shrugged.

"Lou's been worried sick about Sugarfoot," said Ty.

"I know," said Amy. "But it's not like her to get so

moody. That's my job in this family." Amy allowed herself a quick smile.

She came out of the stall and walked Ty to his pickup. He was leaving a couple of hours early to help his mother with a load of errands. Amy gave him a quick kiss and watched him start the engine.

"See you tomorrow!" she called.

Ty waved in return and turned the pickup down the driveway. Amy watched him go, then wandered back to Sugarfoot's stall and looked over the half door. She couldn't help but feel uneasy. Now that she thought about it, the Shetland had been kept out in the pasture ever since the weather had turned warmer. All the horses had been checked every day, at least once, but Sugarfoot was too small to ride and his symptoms might easily have gone unnoticed. What if he'd been developing them for weeks, and Scott's treatment was coming too late? Amy bit her lip, knowing that right now, there was no way to tell.

❧

Fanfare arrived that afternoon in a well-made rented horse trailer driven by Mrs. Hughes. She was the mother of the fallen rider, who was named Kristin. Mrs. Hughes had driven over alone, and as Amy helped her undo the bolts and lower the ramp, she wondered why Kristin hadn't also come. But Amy didn't want to pry; perhaps the girl's broken arm was giving her too much pain to make the journey.

"He's a beauty!" Amy exclaimed when Mrs. Hughes led the paint horse out of the trailer. Fanfare stood on the front yard, his nostrils flaring nervously. He was about sixteen hands — a big, muscular gelding with a white face and a flowing white mane and tail. Amy turned to Lou with a smile. "He reminds me of Albatross."

Albatross was the magnificent horse that had belonged to Huten, an elderly friend of their mother's, who had been something of a mentor to Amy until his death the year before. Fanfare's striking coat had similar markings to Albatross's, and there was something about Fanfare's proud stance that echoed Albatross, too.

Lou nodded and smiled briefly before turning to Mrs. Hughes. "Amy will settle him in," she explained, "if you'd like to come in and sign the paperwork."

Mrs. Hughes handed the lead rope to Amy and gave her an appraising look. "Thank you, Amy," she said, saying good-bye to Fanfare with a final pat. "Are you sure you don't have any questions?" she added, looking a little concerned. Amy was used to seeing owners act this way; there was something unsettling about handing your horse over to someone else — even someone trusted.

"I've already given our team all the details," said Lou

abruptly, starting toward the house. "You stable him at night, don't you?"

"That's right," agreed Mrs. Hughes, falling in step with Lou.

They disappeared into the farmhouse and Amy stared after them, noting that Lou was giving off that air of tension again. But why? Had she and Scott had an argument or something?

Amy sighed and turned her attention to Fanfare, putting her hand on his neck before leading him forward. He shifted away from her, and Amy drew back in surprise.

"Hey, steady, boy," she said softly, studying his features. He had a large, noble head with a Roman nose that gave him an imperious look. His eyes were generous, but the whites were showing as Amy reached her hand up slowly to stroke his nose. His whole body was tense. Amy stroked him gently for a few minutes before asking him to move on.

As they approached the barn, Amy saw Joni coming up the track from the training ring leading Romany.

"So this is Fanfare," said Joni as they passed each other.

"Yes. Isn't he something?"

Joni looked the paint horse over, her head cocked to one side. "How has he been so far?"

"Well, he just got here," Amy said. "He seems a little

high-strung, but I can't see him being too much of a problem. I think I'll give him some walnut remedy first thing. I'd like him to get used to his new environment before we start working on his confidence."

"I'll get some remedy for you," offered Joni. "I'm going up to that barn with Romany anyway."

"That would be great," Amy said gratefully.

She led the horse into the barn and into the second stall. Fanfare was obedient enough, responding to her voice and to pressure on the lead rope, but he snorted nervously as Amy unclipped his halter and closed the door behind them. When Joni reappeared with the little bottle of walnut remedy, Amy added several drops to his water, then let herself out of the stall.

"I think I'll leave him alone for an hour or so, then try some T-touch," Amy told Joni. She made a face. "That means I've got an hour to clean some tack."

"Yeah, and I have an appointment with the muck heap." Joni grinned. "It's beginning to take over the yard. See you later."

When Amy returned to the barn an hour later, she could see that the paint horse hadn't touched his hay net. It looked as if he had drunk some water, though, which meant that the walnut remedy would have started to have some effect. Amy approached the horse quietly and stroked his muzzle before moving back and starting work on his withers, making rhythmic circles up his neck with her fingers.

After half an hour, Amy began to feel surprised at the horse's reaction. True, his muscles were beginning to relax, but she could pick up no sense of enjoyment from him. And he was not making any real connection with her. Fanfare seemed to be accepting her touch, but he was somehow aloof and distant. Amy was reminded of Venture, the police horse that had proved so hard to reach. Acupuncture had worked wonders for him, but he had been suffering from far more than a mere loss of confidence. Perhaps Fanfare just needed time.

After about forty minutes, Amy quietly left the stall and walked back up to the yard. Lou was standing at the farmhouse door, talking to Ty and Joni. As Amy drew closer, she saw that Lou's face was serious and her expressions emphatic. Ty and Joni looked serious as well, listening intently. Amy wondered what Lou was telling them, but when she came within earshot all she heard was Lou saying, "Well, I've got to get back to the office," and she turned and headed indoors.

Joni smiled at Amy and slipped away, leaving Ty alone on the doorstep.

"What was that all about?" Amy asked him.

Ty shrugged. "Just some stuff about billing owners correctly," he replied.

"But Lou does all that herself. How does it concern you and Joni?"

"It doesn't, really. Well, of course it does —" Ty corrected himself, looking uncomfortable. "She just wants to have a sense of what each horse requires."

"But why is she telling you and Joni, and not me?" asked Amy. The memory of the feed order sprang into her mind and she felt stung. "I mean, I'm still at Heartland *now*..."

Ty frowned and touched Amy's shoulder. "It's not like that, Amy. Believe me."

Amy shook her head, unable to dispel her doubts. Still feeling aggrieved, she went to the tack room to collect Spindle's lead rope. To her surprise, it wasn't on its hook. She checked around the tack room and on the metal rings outside, but there was no sign of it. Puzzled, she walked down to the pasture, checking the path in case she'd dropped it.

The mystery was solved quickly. Joni was at the pasture gate fitting Spindle with the lunging cavesson, his halter and lead rope hooked over her shoulder and the lunging whip tucked under her arm.

"Oh!" said Amy in surprise. "What are you doing with Spindle?" she asked Joni, not meaning to sound snippy.

"I was just going to give him a few circuits on the lunge," Joni replied, sounding the slightest bit defensive.

"Alone?" Amy asked, confused.

"That's OK, isn't it?" Joni finished buckling the cavesson and stepped back. "After the last time you guys worked with him, Ty said he was ready."

"You could have checked with me first." The words snapped out more vehemently than Amy meant them to, and Joni stared at her, comprehension dawning on her face.

"I didn't leave you out on purpose." The blond girl's eyes flashed. "You're so defensive lately, Amy! You act as if I'm trying to go behind your back just because you're —"

"Leaving?" Amy interrupted. "Well, just because I *am* leaving doesn't mean *you* can run Heartland now."

Joni looked shocked, and her cheeks blanched. Amy was slightly shocked by her own words. There was an awkward silence. "I'm just doing *my* job, Amy," Joni said eventually. She shrugged off the halter, balanced the whip against the gate, and dumped the lunge line into Amy's hands. Then, without another word, she marched off up the path.

Chapter Four

For the next few days, Amy tried to avoid Joni whenever possible, feeling awkward about their hostile exchange. Amy knew she had lashed out at Joni because of her frustrations over leaving Heartland. She couldn't help but feel that the others on the farm were behaving as if she'd already left, and that was a painful realization to bear.

She decided to cope by burying herself in her work, devoting more attention to Fanfare. By Friday afternoon she was satisfied that she was making some progress with the horse. Fanfare was still strangely distant, but his initial nervousness had subsided. He was calm and responsive on the flat and clearly very well trained, and Amy guessed that it was only when jumping that he had a real problem, since Lou had told her the accident happened at a show. Now that he had settled in, he was ready to start facing his fear.

Amy laid out a course of six low jumps in a figure eight and mounted the big paint horse. She walked Fanfare around to gauge his reaction, stroking his neck to reassure him. The paint horse remained calm and even seemed interested in the brightly colored jumps, arching his neck and pricking his ears as they passed each one.

"Good boy," murmured Amy. "They're not too scary, are they?"

Feeling more confident, Amy nudged him into a trot, then cantered a circle before turning him toward the first jump. Fanfare stretched out his neck, gathered his quarters under him, and popped over it easily. Amy moved on to the next. When Fanfare had jumped all six fences flawlessly, Amy brought him to a halt, feeling puzzled. There had been no signs that the horse had lost any confidence at all in his jumping — no refusals, no fighting, no resistance. But if he'd lost his confidence, how could that be?

Amy rode up to the yard with a suspicion developing in her mind. Fanfare was a fine, well-bred horse that needed plenty of schooling to keep him in shape. Kristin couldn't ride him at the moment, and a good livery stable would be very expensive — more expensive, probably, than Heartland. Had the Hughes family simply gone for a cheap option? Fanfare really didn't seem to have much of a problem — certainly nothing compared to the loss of confidence she had witnessed in other horses that had had similar accidents.

It was an uncomfortable thought, and as she dismounted, Amy tried to find a reason to shake it off. She stood back from the horse for a moment, looking at his big, strong head. He reached down to scratch his foreleg with his teeth, then shook his mane and looked around the yard with what seemed to be a sort of bored detachment.

Ty walked past leading Attitude, a show jumper that had recently developed a rearing problem and whose owners wanted to nip it in the bud. "I saw you putting some jumps up," he commented. "Were they for Fanfare?"

Amy nodded. "He did really well. I'm actually finding him to be something of a mystery. I wish Lou had found out more about his background." She hesitated, wondering whether to express her suspicion. "I'm almost wondering if the Hugheses just sent him to us for some cheap schooling."

Ty looked taken aback. "But they didn't, Amy," he began, then stopped abruptly. "I mean, I doubt it. I think Kristin had a pretty bad accident." He said nothing more.

"But I wonder what it was that freaked Fanfare out about the fall. He clearly wasn't injured. Oh, Ty, I just can't help but feel —" Amy bit her lip. "That Lou isn't telling me the full story for some reason."

Ty fiddled with Attitude's reins, not meeting Amy's gaze. "Maybe you should ask her," he suggested softly.

Amy didn't respond. What she'd been hesitant to confess was that Lou's vagueness about Fanfare spoke to Amy's growing insecurities, her feeling that everyone at Heartland was all too ready to conduct business without her. But she didn't want to bring up her fears with Ty. Not now.

Amy shrugged. "What are you planning on doing with Attitude?" she asked, changing the subject.

Ty stroked the bay gelding's neck. "Some flat work in the school, I think," he said. "I want to pinpoint what triggers the rearing. I get the feeling it's not fear, more a way of telling his rider when he's unhappy. I guess he didn't get his name for nothing."

Amy smiled. The first thing Attitude had done upon arriving at Heartland was to tear down his hay net and trample the hay into his bedding. Attitude certainly had a feisty side — unlike the paint horse. He was still standing patiently, waiting for Amy to remove his tack.

"You'd better get him down there," she said. "He's not as easy-going as this fellow."

Ty nodded and grinned. "See you later." He clicked his tongue at Attitude and led the horse down the path.

Amy went around Fanfare's side to unbuckle his girth, but as she lifted the saddle flap, she paused. The jumping session hadn't been that long; the big gelding had barely begun to sweat. It wouldn't do him any harm to get more exercise, Amy reflected. Maybe if she took him out on the trails, she would be able to connect more deeply with Fanfare and get a better sense of what was really wrong; perhaps it wasn't a jumping problem after all.

It was a warm afternoon, and Amy decided to take a bottle of water with her. She slipped Fanfare's reins over his head, tied them loosely to a metal ring, and ran quickly into the tack room, where she almost bumped into Joni, who was coming out with Moonstone's tack.

"Oh, hi," said Amy, stepping aside and feeling awkward.

Joni smiled sheepishly, and Amy realized how foolish it was for her to stay upset with Joni. The other girl meant well, and Amy hated there to be any hostility in the stable, even if she was still feeling weird about her imminent departure.

"It's a scorcher today," Amy commented, hoping to break the ice. "I'm just getting a water bottle to take out on the trails."

Joni smiled again, and this time she seemed more relaxed. "That sounds good. Who are you taking?"

"Fanfare," said Amy, turning on the tack room tap and holding a bottle under the faucet.

Joni stood very still, clutching the bridle to her chest.

Amy screwed on the bottle cap and walked toward her, expecting her to lead the way outdoors. But Joni didn't move.

"Are you OK?" Amy asked curiously.

Joni flushed. "It's just . . ." She shifted the saddle a little higher up her forearm and cleared her throat. "It's just that I don't think you should ride Fanfare out on the trails."

Amy stared at her. "What?"

"Amy, listen, I just think —"

"Joni, what are you saying?" Anger welled up inside Amy, threatening to explode like a firework. So much for patching things up with Joni. "You can't just order me —"

Joni shook her head, her expression anxious. "I'm not," she said. "Please, Amy. I know this is coming off badly, but — I just get the impression that Fanfare's unpredictable," Joni said helplessly. "And when I rode Mischief out earlier this week, there was a log across the track . . ."

Amy tried to suppress her anger, but it was difficult. Joni's comment about Fanfare felt like the icing on the cake. "I think I know what I'm doing," Amy spoke quietly. "I'm the one who's been riding Fanfare all week."

Joni looked upset but said nothing. Amy headed for the door, and the other girl stepped aside for her to pass. Swinging the water bottle strap over her shoulder, Amy untied Fanfare's reins and mounted.

"See you later," she told Joni coolly, nudging the gelding forward.

Joni seemed glued to the spot. When Amy glanced back on her way out of the yard, she was still standing in the tack room doorway with Moonstone's tack in her arms.

❧

Once they were walking up the path beneath the trees, Amy felt herself calm down. She felt bad for snapping at Joni — she felt so unlike herself lately. But it *had* been sort of rude on Joni's part to so abruptly recommend that Amy not take Fanfare out. Amy still bristled slightly at the memory.

Fanfare climbed steadily upward, his ears pricked, walking briskly. A bird flew out in front of them and the horse shied, jerking backward. Amy soothed him, stroking his neck, and after a couple of minutes he walked forward again. It was the first sign of any real nervousness since the day he'd arrived — but it was hardly surprising. Many horses would have reacted the same way.

Amy urged Fanfare into a trot when the path leveled out. This path that led up to beautiful Clairdale Ridge held so many memories for Amy . . . riding with her mom, and with Ty and Soraya. Riding Sundance, Pegasus, Storm, and so many other horses that had come and gone, as the trees changed to green, red, and gold at different times of the year.

When they reached the top of the ridge, Amy reined in Fanfare and looked down over the view, feeling the breeze on her face and taking a swig of water from the bottle. As she replaced the bottle cap and turned Fanfare onto the path once more, she reflected that the paint horse was responding to her riding much as he did in the school. He still seemed as relaxed as ever, even after spooking at the bird.

As the path wound back down the ridge, Amy came across a fallen tree toward the bottom, barring the way back to Heartland. *So that's what Joni was talking about,* she thought. Its branches spiked upward violently, making the log impossible to jump. Amy reined in Fanfare and wondered what to do. They had been out for well over an hour, and the quickest way back would be to take a slightly more roundabout path to the road. She generally avoided going that way; it meant joining the road for about five hundred yards. It was a narrow stretch, and not ideal for riding. She decided to try it anyway.

They turned onto the paved road. Fanfare immediately quickened his stride, and Amy had to hold him back with her seat and reins. She was surprised — it was the typical reaction of a horse who knew he was nearing home, but Fanfare had never been on this route before.

"Steady, Fanfare!" she murmured as a car approached. The gelding seemed in more of a hurry than ever. As the car slowed down, he crabbed sideways, twisting his head. Once the car had crept past safely, Amy put her hand on his neck and realized he was sweating. Now the paint horse seemed truly nervous. And Amy felt a rush of nerves herself.

As another car approached and the gelding grew more agitated, Amy suddenly realized that this was where Fanfare's problem must lie — out on the roads. Did Lou know that? If so, why hadn't she told Amy?

The car passed without mishap, but Fanfare broke into a jog and sawed at the bit, throwing his head up to gain control. Amy fought to restrain him, her arms aching as he snatched at the reins over and over again. All of Amy's concentration was focused on the distressed, struggling horse, and she was barely aware of the vehicle coming at them around the corner, or the ominous rumbling like thunder of enormous wheels.

Fanfare saw it before she did. As the logging truck roared up the hill and lumbered into sight, he gave a shrill whinny of fear and reared up, his hooves flailing in the air. Amy had no time to react. She felt herself being thrown forward, losing control. And all she saw was a blur of wheels and the flurry of Fanfare's white face and tail as she crashed down, down, down.

Then everything went black.

Chapter Five

❦

Amy was in the truck. A terrified horse was in the back, thrashing the walls of the trailer with his hooves. Thunder boomed overhead, and rain lashed the windshield. It was getting darker. They were approaching a tunnel of trees that lined the road, a dark, dark tunnel, and the horse in the trailer was getting frantic. The trees were all around them now, scraping the roof and looming overhead.

Lightning lit up the road, lit up the trees, and the air was filled with a cracking sound. Amy felt a terrible, sickening lurch and looked around desperately for her mother. "Mom!" she tried to scream, but her voice couldn't form the word.

The truck was skidding. There was nothing she could do. Amy saw a flash of green, wet leaves. She was pinned to her seat, and as the tree fell, her ears were full of the stallion screaming.

"Amy!"

Amy turned frantically, reaching for her mother, her fingers grasping thin air . . .

"Amy, shh. It's OK. Wake up."

Amy blinked her eyes open, her heart thudding. "Mom?"

A familiar blond-haired figure was gazing down at her. *Not Mom,* Amy realized. *Lou.* "Amy, Mom's not here. You're at home. You had an accident," Lou said softly.

Amy stared up at her sister, not comprehending. "Mom's in the truck," she mumbled. "You have to get to her. She's hurt. And it's my fault. I shouldn't have made her go . . ."

Suddenly, Jack's taut, worried face appeared beside Lou's. "Honey, it's Grandpa. Relax. You're home, at Heartland."

"But where's Mom? And Spartan?" Amy struggled to sit up. She looked around, utterly disoriented. She was on the sofa in the living room at Heartland. Lou and Grandpa were leaning over her, their faces very pale. Amy had no idea what time — or day — it was. Pain shot through her head and shoulder, and she fell back on the sofa again.

Lou knelt down and took Amy's hands in her own, her

expression serious. "Amy, listen to me. Mom's not here. That accident happened a long time ago."

"What do you mean?" Amy whispered, trying to piece her jumbled thoughts together.

"You just had a bad fall," said Lou, her voice trembling. "You were riding Fanfare out on the trails, and he threw you on the road. Do you remember?"

Amy's head was thudding and she gripped Lou's hand with her last ounce of strength. The image of a horse's noble white face flashed through her mind. She frowned. But Spartan's face wasn't white. Amy shut her eyes, and the tunnel of dark trees closed around her again.

When she opened her eyes again there were strangers in the room, wearing green overalls. Paramedics. She tried to sit up, but now she felt dizzy and sick.

"Can't go to the hospital," she murmured. "Spartan needs me. He's scared, so scared."

She heard Lou talking to the paramedics. "She's really confused," Amy heard Lou say. "Our mom died in a car accident, and Amy was with her when it happened. I think she's confusing everything in her head. Does she really need to go to the hospital?"

Amy looked up and saw a dark-haired woman in green overalls smiling down at her. "Amy," the woman was saying, "how many fingers can you see?" She held her hand close to Amy's face with some of the fingers curled down.

"Three," Amy said faintly.

"And now?"

"Four."

"Good."

The woman shone a bright light into Amy's eyes.

"Now, grip my finger." Amy followed the woman's instructions instinctively. She moved her arms and legs and answered simple questions — her name, where she lived, how old she was. She felt that the quicker she got through the exam, the sooner she could be out looking for her mom and Spartan.

"OK," the woman said, turning to Lou. "She can stay here as long as she gets complete rest. If she starts vomiting, develops a severe headache, or if any of her current symptoms get worse, call us immediately."

Amy felt a blanket of sleep drawing over her, but she fought against it. She couldn't fall asleep now. There was too much to do. She had to get back out there. She had to find her mom and the horse with the white face. Then Amy felt Grandpa's cool hand on her forehead, and she couldn't fight the longing to sleep anymore.

When she awoke, the room seemed darker. Lou was sitting next to her on a chair. Her sister smiled, and Amy stared at her, still trying to piece together what had happened.

Lou's eyes filled with sadness as she accurately read

Amy's bewildered expression. "Amy, you have to listen carefully. Tell me if you understand. The accident with Mom happened more than two years ago."

The words fell like icicles into Amy's heart as comprehension began to dawn at last.

"I'm so sorry, sweetheart," Lou murmured. "Don't you remember?"

Amy stared at her sister as something shifted inside her mind, like snow settling after an avalanche. She felt a tide of grief well up inside her, and a tear ran down her cheek. "Mom," she whispered, feeling utterly lost. "Two years ago . . ."

Lou shook her head, stroking Amy's forehead. "Amy, I'm so sorry."

Amy lay in silence for several minutes. Her mother had died two years ago. She knew that. But her grief felt so fresh and raw that she thought her heart would break. She felt as if the accident with her mother had happened only moments before. She gazed at Lou's face, searching for any sign of comfort.

"Everything's fine," Lou whispered. "You're safe now. You're going to be OK."

Amy swallowed. "But there was a horse . . ."

"Yes. You had a fall on Fanfare."

"Spartan. Wasn't it Spartan?" Amy asked through her fog of confusion.

Lou shook her head again, and Amy frowned, biting her lip. "The horse with the white face? Fanfare?"

"That's right."

"But, Lou, what about Spartan?"

Lou didn't answer. She went to the table and picked up a glass of water, which she handed to Amy, carefully folding her sister's fingers around it as if Amy were a little girl. Amy took a sip and realized how parched her throat felt. She gulped down some more.

Lou sat down again and held Amy's hand. "Amy, work with me here?" Lou pleaded softly. "Do you remember riding Fanfare?"

Amy closed her eyes. There was a tunnel of trees — wasn't there? There was a frightened horse, and she'd thought he was behind her, in a truck, but, suddenly, she wasn't sure. She was rising, then falling, falling, with the flash of white face in front of her as everything went dark.

"He got scared," she said slowly.

"Yes, that's right," Lou encouraged her. "You were on the road, and Fanfare got scared."

"The trailer . . ." Amy began. Something wasn't right. The horse wasn't in the trailer. He was there, out on the road.

"Take your time," Lou said.

"Where is Fanfare?" Amy whispered.

"He's here, at Heartland," said Lou. "Ty caught him.

He was still on the road. His saddle had slipped and he'd broken his reins, but he wasn't injured. Just very wound up."

Amy tried to digest this new piece of information, feeling confused. A horse loose on the road, not in the trailer. A white face and a sensation of falling. And her mother hadn't been there — and wasn't here now.

Suddenly, Ty came into the room. At the sight of him, Amy's heart surged. *Ty.* He would make everything better.

Ty kissed Amy on the cheek, then drew up a chair next to Lou.

"How is he?" Lou asked Ty quietly.

Ty shook his head. "Pretty wired. He wouldn't even take any rescue remedy. I put some in his water and put an orange bulb in his stall. Hopefully, he'll start calming down now." Then he turned to Amy, his green eyes dark with worry. "More important, how is she holding up?" he whispered, glancing back at Lou.

"Not good," Lou murmured. "She's had a concussion. She remembers most things, but she keeps mixing up Fanfare and Spartan."

"*Spartan?*" Ty's voice was full of disbelief — and sorrow. "God, Lou. It must have brought her back . . ."

Don't talk about me like I'm not here! Amy longed to cry. But she was too weak to speak. She closed her eyes, and before sleep overcame her, she thought of her mother once more. *Oh, Mom.* Suddenly, Amy longed for her like never before.

㋢

When Amy awoke from a deep, dreamless sleep, there was sunlight streaming into the room. She was still on the sofa, but there were several blankets over her and a glass of water on the coffee table beside her. She squinted in the sunlight. The living room got the sun only in the morning. So it must be morning.

There were sounds coming from the kitchen — voices and the faint whistle of the kettle. Breakfast time? Amy frowned. What on earth was she doing here? Had she fallen asleep watching TV? She needed to get up and head onto the yard.

She swung her legs off the sofa and tried to sit up. All at once the room began to swim and a dull thudding pain shot through her head, making her cry out loud.

"Amy!" Lou rushed in from the kitchen.

Amy lay back against the cushions. "I'm fine," she said. "It's just my head . . ."

Amy had never seen Lou look so worried. "Amy, you were hurt badly yesterday. The doctors say you have to lie still."

Doctors. Hurt badly. Slowly, the fragmented memories filtered back. She'd been in an accident. She'd crashed in a truck, and her mom had been hurt. No, that had happened years ago. Amy felt another wave of grief wash over her as she forced herself to accept her mother's absence.

There had been another accident yesterday. The horse, not Spartan but Fanfare, had been frightened, really frightened.

Lou made sure Amy was resting properly, then went to get her a mug of weak tea. "There's plenty of sugar in it," said Lou, returning. "You should eat something, too. I've brought you one of Nancy's honey and pecan muffins."

"Thanks." Amy reached for the muffin and took a bite. It tasted like sawdust and she chewed it mechanically. She had no appetite whatsoever. At last she managed to swallow, and put the rest of the muffin back on the plate.

"How are you feeling?" asked Lou. "Any better? You would've slept right through, but the paramedics said I should wake you up every couple of hours because of your concussion. Do you even remember me coming in?"

Lou's voice sounded as if it was coming from miles away. Amy remembered having a difficult conversation with her sister. "We were talking about Spartan . . ." Amy mumbled.

Lou nodded, looking hopeful. "You thought you'd been with Spartan. But you were with Fanfare this time. You realize that, right, Amy? You weren't riding Spartan," she said. "You were riding Fanfare. Spartan came to Heartland a long time ago. You helped him and he went back to his owner."

Amy nodded at Lou. "Fanfare . . ." She whispered, remembering the horse's fear on the road. "I have to see him," Amy said, throwing off the blankets.

"No," Lou said firmly. "I'm glad you're remembering things better, but you're still in no condition to go outside. You have to lie still for at least another twenty-four hours, and you can't start work again for a week. Fanfare's fine. He's being taken care of. You don't need to worry about a thing."

Amy obediently took a sip of tea, and Lou waited until she had sunk back against the cushions before standing up again. "I just have to make a couple of phone calls in the office," she said. "I'll be back in a few minutes."

Amy watched her sister leave the room. There was no sound from the kitchen now. Everyone must have gone out. In the stillness of the sunny room, the memory of her mother flooded back, and with it the newly opened wound of Amy's grief. She held her head between her hands and shut her eyes.

"Not now. Not now," she muttered to herself. She pushed the pain away and focused on Fanfare. The urge to see the frightened horse was rising again. Amy opened her eyes, then slowly, carefully sat up on the sofa. Her head didn't feel too bad. She leaned her hand on the coffee table and gently levered herself upward.

A wave of nausea hit her and she clutched the arm of the sofa. She stood still for a few seconds, taking deep breaths. The room was spinning, but she found that if she tilted her head in one position, it slowed down. Tentatively, she took a few steps forward and made it to the kitchen door. She peered around it to make sure that it was empty. With slow, even strides, she walked to the front door and opened it. No matter what, she needed to see Fanfare.

Just then, Lou's cry erupted behind her.

"Amy! No!"

Amy turned around, which dizzied her even more. She staggered as Lou hurried over to the front door and grabbed her arm.

"Amy, what do you think you're doing?" Lou's voice was tight with worry and anger. "You could really hurt yourself. You *have* to lie down."

"Lou, please," Amy protested. "I want to see Fanfare. That truck — he was so scared." She leaned on Lou's arm, memories clearer now. She hadn't been in a truck — she'd been riding. She remembered the feel of the horse beneath her and his sweaty flank. "I took him onto the road, and he started to panic."

Anguish filled Lou's eyes. "If I'd known you were

taking him on the road, I would have never . . ." She trailed off.

"Why?" Amy asked, suddenly feeling more alert. "Did you — know something about his fear?"

Lou's face was very white. "Yes, Amy," she said in a shaky voice. "There's something I have to tell you. But please lie down first."

Amy relented and let Lou steer her back onto the sofa. Her shoulder and head were throbbing, and it was a relief to feel the cushions supporting her once more. But her curiosity — and a sense of growing anxiety — made her forget her pain for a moment.

Lou sat down next to her and took a deep breath. "I'm sorry," she began. "I thought it was for the best."

"What was for the best?" Amy asked, feeling confused again.

Lou looked down at her hands. I didn't tell you the full truth about Fanfare. "Kristin's accident wasn't a fall," she said in a low voice. "She was in the cab of a horse trailer. She and her father were driving back from a show down in North Carolina and they hit a storm."

Amy's mouth went dry.

Lou continued. "The wind blew a sheet of timber into their path and it crashed into the cab, pretty much destroying it." She bit her lip.

Amy gasped. The flashbacks to the crash with her mom had been starting to fade, but now they came surging back. She could see her mom's white knuckles gripping the steering wheel and the flashes of lightning that lit up the narrow road. She could hear the thunder of hooves against the trailer and the panic-stricken screams of the stallion inside. Worst of all, she could feel the truck entering that nightmarish tunnel and their hopeless slide toward the falling tree. She closed her eyes and gripped Lou's arm.

"I knew it would upset you," Lou whispered. "That's why I didn't want to tell you. I — I'll stop now. You need to rest."

"No! Don't stop, Lou. I have to know." Amy opened her eyes again and gazed at Lou steadily. As difficult as this was, Amy was desperate to know the whole truth. "Go on," she whispered.

Lou hesitated, then cleared her throat. "Kristin was lucky to escape with a broken arm, but her dad was injured much more seriously. In fact, he's still in the hospital." Lou's voice began to shake again, and she paused to take a deep breath. "He might be paralyzed for life," she finished.

"And Fanfare?" Amy whispered.

"He was in the trailer," Lou told her. "When the timber crashed into the cab, the whole thing fell over. Fanfare was stuck inside. He wasn't injured, but of course he's developed a terror of any sort of traffic."

Amy stared straight ahead, barely able to comprehend

what Lou had told her. It seemed almost beyond belief that another family and another horse had suffered such a similar fate. Could it be? Fanfare, Kristin, and Kristin's father had suffered what Amy and Spartan had on that terrible night — the night when she had lost her mother forever.

Chapter Six

❧

Amy and Lou sat in silence for a few moments. Amy shook her head, trying to expel the memories of her mother's death from her mind. But she was also being nagged by another kind of pain — the realization that Lou had kept the truth about Fanfare from her.

"So, you knew about this all along?" Amy asked quietly. "And everyone else?"

Lou hid her face in her hands. "Yes." She looked up with tears in her eyes. "Everyone knew. I asked them not to tell you."

Amy felt as if she'd been struck. *Everyone*. Grandpa. Ty. Scott. She swallowed. "Even Joni?" she whispered.

Lou nodded, confirming Amy's worst fears. She'd been the only one in the dark.

Suddenly, it all made sense: Lou's tense behavior all

week. Ty not revealing anything about Fanfare. And Joni trying to stop Amy from going on the trails. All of them had been in on it, watching her work blindly with a horse she didn't understand. How could they have done that to her? How had they all decided she wouldn't be able to cope? Did they think she wasn't strong enough? Amy felt a rush of hurt and fury.

"Amy?" Lou's fingers were touching her arm.

"You should have told me," Amy burst out. "You all stood by and watched as I struggled to reach Fanfare." Tears began to trickle down her face. "And I'm mad at myself, too. I can't believe I didn't sense something had happened to Fanfare. So much for me having a way with horses."

A sense of guilty horror welled up inside as Amy remembered what she'd been thinking about the Hughes's reasons for sending Fanfare to Heartland. *Some cheap schooling!* How had she got it so terribly, tragically wrong?

Lou shook her head as Amy's tears began to flow freely. "Amy, of course you have a way with horses. You're more gifted than all of us put together. How were you to know Fanfare's trauma? It's *my* fault. And everyone feels terrible. Joni even offered to resign." Lou's voice broke, and Amy looked up through her tears.

"She blames herself for letting you go out on Fanfare," Lou continued. "She knew you might have to take him on the road because of the fallen tree. But she kept quiet because I had asked her to. I can't allow her to take any blame."

Amy was still trying to process all the information. Her tears slowed and she wiped her cheeks, aware that her head was throbbing painfully. She placed her palm on her forehead, wincing.

"This is too much for you now," Lou said. "You need to rest." She paused. "I'm so, so sorry, Amy. Please believe me."

Amy nodded, but Lou's words seemed distant. All that mattered was that she — and the others — hadn't trusted Amy enough. They hadn't had faith in her. *But maybe I'm* not *strong enough,* Amy realized, feeling how exhausted she was.

"Can you help me get up to my room?" Amy asked, barely able to meet Lou's gaze.

"Of course. You'll have to take it slowly, though," said Lou. "No sudden movements."

Amy eased herself off the sofa and, with Lou's help, made it slowly up the stairs. Once they were in Amy's own room, Lou eased her onto her bed.

"Should I help you get into your pajamas?" Lou asked.

Amy looked down. She was still wearing her riding clothes from the day before, though someone had taken her boots off. She shook her head. "I can get changed myself," she said firmly.

"Are you sure?"

Amy looked at her sister. "I am," she said, "And, right now, I think I just need to be alone."

❧

When Lou had gone downstairs, Amy slowly changed into her pajamas, then lay back on the bed. She stared at the ceiling, massaging her bruised shoulder with her fingertips. It was late morning by now. Everyone was already out on the yard. Without her. Just as Amy had feared — they were all ready for her to leave. That was why they hadn't told her about Fanfare. Not even Ty.

A wave of misery swept over Amy and she began to sob. Fanfare's trauma *was* a reminder of Spartan and the accident that had killed Marion. Perhaps she would never be able to face something so personal. As Amy wept, she felt the old guilt and sorrow from two years ago. If only Amy hadn't made Marion go out there in that terrible storm . . .

"Oh, Mom," Amy sobbed. "Mom, I'm so sorry. I wish you were here."

Eventually, her tears subsided and she drifted into sleep. She was vaguely aware of Lou coming in with a tray of food, which she placed by Amy's bedside. Amy dozed on. Sleep was a safer place than the waking world, and she clung on to it for as long as she could. When she finally awoke, dusk was falling. Her headache was much better, and even her shoulder ached less acutely. She stood slowly, relieved that the dizziness had passed, and went into the bathroom to shower.

When she was finished, Amy stood before her bedroom mirror clad in a towel, assessing her bruises. Her left shoulder was turning an angry shade of purple, but otherwise she had only a small scrape on her knee. She had been lucky — a fall onto a blacktop road could have led to much worse. She dressed in clean clothes, then propped herself up against her pillows and picked up a horse magazine. The letters danced on the page in front of her, so she closed the magazine and stared at the cover. A photo of a girl stroking a beautiful palomino pony. They seemed so peaceful and serene, as if tragedy had never touched them.

There was a soft knock on the door and Amy looked up.

"It's only me." Lou opened the door a crack. "May I come in?"

"Sure," Amy replied curtly.

Lou came in and looked at the tray. "You didn't eat lunch," she said, sitting down on the bed. "How are you feeling? I heard you taking a shower."

"I'm fine. I slept a lot." Amy studied her fingernails.

"I have some news about Sugarfoot," Lou told her. "He tested positive for EPM."

Amy looked up.

"Scott started his treatment," Lou continued. "He

thinks we've caught the symptoms early enough. He says it'll be a long treatment, but we should see signs of improvement soon."

Amy smiled wanly. She was relieved to know that the Shetland would pull through. But she wished she had been there to receive Scott's diagnosis herself. And she was still feeling hurt and resentful toward both Lou and Scott . . . and everyone.

Lou bit her lip. "I thought that news would cheer you a little," she said softly. "Listen, Amy, if you want to talk about it —"

Amy shook her head sharply. "There's nothing more to say," she replied abruptly.

Lou sighed. "You should come down for supper," she said gently. "You must be starving."

It was true. Amy felt her stomach rumble, but the last thing she wanted to do was go down and face everyone. "Could you bring something up here?" she asked.

Lou hesitated. "Everyone wants to see you, Amy."

"I can't," Amy said.

"OK. I'll see what Nancy's cooking." Lou stood, picking up the lunch tray. "You're looking a lot better," she added as she walked to the door. "You've got some color in your cheeks."

She shut the door behind her with a soft click. Amy lay back on her pillows for a few moments, then picked up the magazine again. Its cheerful glossy pictures quickly irritated her and she cast it aside. The catalog for Virginia Tech was lying on her desk, so she reached across for that and flicked through, looking blankly at photos of the college buildings and dorms, trying to imagine herself in the strange new environment. Thinking about school somehow felt easier than dealing with what was happening at Heartland. For the first time, Amy felt eager to escape to a place where she could start anew. Where nobody knew her past.

❧

Half an hour later, there was another knock on the door and Jack came in, carrying a tray. "Hi, honey," he greeted her. "I've brought you some chicken pot pie."

It smelled delicious, and Amy felt her stomach squeeze with hunger. "Thanks, Grandpa."

Jack handed her the tray. "How's the head?" he asked, sitting on the bed.

"Better." Amy picked up the fork and started to eat. As always, Nancy's cooking was wonderful. Grandpa watched her dig in, and Amy noticed he was smiling.

"Well, it's good to see you have an appetite," he commented warmly. "Maybe you'll feel well enough to come down tomorrow? We're all missing you."

Amy glanced up at her grandfather's kind eyes. Grandpa hadn't thought it wise to tell her about Fanfare. She wanted to ask him about it, but she couldn't bring herself to — the hurt was too sharp. She blinked back tears and nodded. "Maybe."

"I'll let you finish," he said, standing. "Is there anything else you'd like? Ice cream for dessert?"

Amy shook her head, and Grandpa went downstairs. Suddenly, her appetite disappeared. She set the pot pie aside and rummaged in her pocket for a tissue. Grandpa must have seen the college catalog on her lap, but he hadn't even asked her about it. No one seemed to understand how she was feeling. It seemed incredible that she could feel so lonely among the people she loved most in the world.

❦

The next morning, Lou brought Amy a cup of coffee and a muffin, then went back down to the office. Amy drank the coffee in bed and flicked through some information brochures Virginia Tech had recently mailed her. From time to time, she would hear the sound of horses' hooves on the yard, so she turned on the radio to block out the noise. Whenever she thought of Fanfare, a sense of dread ran through her. It was probably better for the horse if he didn't see her. All she had done was add to his trauma by going on the road; it would be easier if the others treated him without her.

The day passed slowly. When Lou poked her head in to say that Ty wanted to come up and see her, Amy felt a pang of longing to see her boyfriend. But she told Lou she'd rather wait until she was feeling better. The fact that Ty, out of everyone, had kept Fanfare's history from her was the most hurtful. Amy didn't know how she'd react when she saw him. She'd rather put it off.

Later that afternoon, Amy got a call on her cell phone. It was Soraya.

"Amy!" Soraya exclaimed. "Matt told me what happened. How are you? I got so worried!"

"It sounds worse than it was," Amy lied. It was such a relief to talk to someone who hadn't been involved in the Fanfare secret. "I'm still in bed, though. My head feels sort of weird. Foggy."

"Matt said you have a concussion. Are you sure you're all right otherwise?"

"All in one piece, more or less," Amy replied, her spirits lifted by Soraya's sympathetic tone. "No bones broken or anything."

"What about the horse?"

Amy hesitated, wondering how much Soraya had been told about Fanfare. *Did she know, too?* Amy wondered, then dismissed her flash of paranoia. "He'll be fine," she managed to say. "He's doing OK, too."

"Oh, right. You probably can't work yet," said Soraya. "It must be awful for you sitting inside all alone. I don't know if you're up for it, but how about I pick you up this evening and we go see a movie?"

"Pick me up?" Amy echoed. At the idea of getting into a car, her palms grew clammy.

"Of course," Soraya said, "Unless you're not feeling steady enough for a movie yet. We could go tomorrow."

Amy considered it. It *would* be good to get away from Heartland for a few hours. To escape from all the memories, and from the shadow of everyone's unspoken guilt. She took a deep breath. "Tomorrow sounds good," she said.

"Great," Soraya said. "But call me in the morning if you're still not feeling well."

"Thanks, Soraya," Amy replied, touched by her friend's kindness.

"Otherwise I'll come pick you up at about two. Take care."

"I will." Amy clicked her phone shut, and for the first time in two days, she smiled.

Soraya arrived promptly at two the next day. Amy had spent the morning in bed, and had taken her time getting ready. Her head still felt heavy, as if someone had placed an unsteady lead weight in the middle of it, but it was better than the day before. She chose clothes that she would never wear on the yard — her best jeans and a bright blue sequined T-shirt that Lou had given her for her birthday. As she rubbed a smudge of pink gloss onto her lips, she reflected that it might be nice to doll herself up more often, once she got to college. *Though Ty says he likes me just the way I am on the yard*, Amy thought. But thinking of Ty made her stomach ache.

She heard Soraya honk her horn in the front yard and scooped up a tote bag, then made her way cautiously down the stairs. She hoped she'd be able to leave without seeing anyone. But when she entered the kitchen, Joni was making herself a sandwich at the table. She looked up, and Amy braced herself.

"Hi, Amy. It's so good to see you." Joni smiled, but her expression was wary, as if she expected Amy to snap at her.

Amy forced a smile. There was a tense pause. Joni buttered her slices of bread while Amy fiddled with her bag.

"Lou said you're going out for a drive," Joni said at last. "It's a nice day for it. Maybe you'd like to have a look around the yard when you get back?"

Amy flinched. Joni said it so casually, almost as if nothing had happened. Clearly, she didn't understand how Amy was feeling in the slightest. She made it sound like she was a visitor! "I'll see," Amy managed to reply, her throat tight.

Joni's face fell. "Well, the horses are missing you."

Amy said nothing. She watched as Joni folded a slice of cheese onto one slice of bread.

"You must be curious to know how they're all doing," Joni added, addressing her sandwich. "Scott tested the other horses for EPM, and they're all clear. Sugarfoot's on the medication now, so he should start getting better really soon. Scott thinks he must have brought the infection with him from where he lived before. Moonstone's doing well, and Ty says she can go back home in the next few days. We've been having some problems with Attitude, though. He's one difficult horse. He just knows he's acting up and he seems to love it . . ." Her voice trailed off as she lifted her gaze to meet Amy's.

Amy nodded. She had barely heard a word. All she noticed was what Joni had left out. Spindleberry. Fanfare. The accident.

"Sounds like everything's under control," Amy said, and numbly turned away before Joni could find a response. She stepped outside, the bright sunlight momentarily blinding her.

"Amy!" Soraya called. She rushed over, engulfing Amy in a big hug. "How are you? Are you still OK to go out? We don't have to, you know."

Amy returned the hug. "I'm fine. It's so good to see you." She adjusted her bag on her shoulder and followed Soraya quickly to her car without even looking at the stable block. She hesitated a heartbeat before climbing into the passenger seat.

Soraya seemed to pick up on her hesitation. "Are you sure you're all right with this?" she asked again, climbing in beside her. "Your head doesn't hurt too much or anything?"

"No, I'm much better. Honestly. I just want to get out of the house a little. Though a movie might be a little long," she admitted.

"That's cool," Soraya said, starting the engine. "We can just drive around and catch up a little."

Amy was silent, her hands in her lap, as Soraya turned the car around. "I chatted with Ty while I was waiting for you," Soraya said once they were heading down the driveway. "I was telling him about my party. I've picked a date for later in the summer." She paused. "But Ty didn't seem all that psyched, to be honest. He must still be worried about you. He seemed kind of quiet."

"I guess," Amy said lamely. She wasn't about to tell Soraya that she hadn't spoken to Ty since the accident. She looked out the window at the trees flashing past. Her pulse quickened.

Soraya gave her a sidelong glance. "I meant to tell you how good you look," she said. "You're a little paler, but I love that top. And you should wear lip gloss more often."

Amy smiled, and they drove along in silence for a few moments. Soraya turned the radio on, then gave an impish grin. "So, what do you think of the new car? How's my driving?"

Amy wished she hadn't asked. All at once, she became acutely aware of the road and of the traffic whizzing past them on the other side. She gripped her seat and concentrated on the car's interior instead, looking at the glossy dashboard and Soraya's bright red seat covers. "It's so nice," she said shakily. "And you're a really good driver."

"Thanks," Soraya said. "It's fun to drive this car."

Amy tried to tell herself that being in a car was perfectly safe. It was a sunny day. Soraya *was* a good driver. This had nothing to do with what had happened to Fanfare. Or to what had happened to her mother. If only her heart would stop racing. She looked straight ahead, forcing herself to relax.

She saw the truck pulling out of an intersection up ahead before Soraya did.

"Soraya!" Amy's near-hysterical scream sounded foreign to her own ears.

Soraya gasped and braked violently, throwing them both forward against their seat belts.

Amy felt all her control dissolve. She began to sob, big, tearing sobs that racked her body.

"Oh, no, Amy! Why are you crying?" Soraya exclaimed. Amy was only vaguely aware of the car pulling over and Soraya turning off the engine.

Amy couldn't stop crying. "Hush, hush," Soraya said,

her voice frightened. She put her arm around Amy's shoulder. "Amy, please. We're fine. I just braked suddenly. Is that why you're so upset?"

"But you didn't see it — that truck . . ."

"Of course I saw it. It was way ahead of us. It was your scream that scared me."

Amy wiped her eyes. "I'm sorry, Soraya," she whispered. "Ever since my accident on Fanfare, I've been having all these flashbacks . . ."

"Oh, Amy." Soraya gently stroked Amy's hair. "You mean about you . . . and your mom?"

Amy nodded as Soraya handed her a tissue. "Yes." She sniffled. "But there's more. It turns out that before Fanfare came to Heartland, he'd been in the exact same kind of accident."

Soraya swallowed, her brown eyes full of concern. "Amy, I wish you had told me. I'd never have suggested we go for a drive . . ."

"I just wanted to pretend everything was normal," Amy said, blowing her nose. "But I still have a lot of recovering to do."

"Let me take you home," Soraya offered gently. She seemed unsure about what to say further. She drove back to Heartland at a snail's pace, double-checking at every intersection before making a move. Amy sat quietly, taking deep, calming breaths. At last they turned up the driveway, and she heaved a sigh of relief.

Ty was sweeping the front yard and looked up as the car came to a stop outside the farmhouse. Amy got out, feeling sick and dizzy, and found that her legs were trembling. She leaned on the car for a moment.

Ty came striding over, his brow furrowed. "Amy. Are you OK?" He reached for her, but Amy stepped away from him.

"You *both* look really pale," Ty said when Soraya emerged. "What happened, Soraya?"

"Well . . . we saw this truck," Soraya began. "I braked hard. That's kind of it, but . . ."

Ty nodded, swallowing hard. "I get it," he said. He turned to Amy again, but she was already heading inside. She collapsed on the sofa, grabbing a cushion and hugging it close to her chest. Ty and Soraya walked in.

"I should go," Soraya said awkwardly.

Amy smiled weakly. "I'm fine. Promise," she said.

Soraya straightened up. "OK. I'm sorry about what happened."

Amy shook her head. "I'm fine."

After Soraya had left, Ty sat beside Amy on the sofa. They were silent.

Amy heard Soraya's car start up and head off down the driveway. She rested her cheek on the cushion, playing with a tassel and trying to fight back the tears that were building.

Ty cleared his throat. "Can I get you anything?"

Amy shook her head. "No. Thanks."

"I'm so glad to finally see you." Ty's voice was choked with emotion. "I wanted to talk to you about . . . I'm really sorry about what happened."

Amy put the cushion down and sat up. "Ty," she began, her voice breaking. "You knew all along what had happened to Fanfare and you didn't tell me."

"But I didn't agree with Lou. I thought you should know."

"Oh, *did* you?" cried Amy. She sprang to her feet, ignoring the strange sensation the sudden movement caused in her head. "Well, it's too late, isn't it?" She glared at him through the tears that had started to flow.

Ty leaned forward and rested his elbows on his knees. He stared at his hands for a moment. "Amy, listen. Nobody ever thought this would happen. And Lou's my boss —"

"And, supposedly, *I'm* your girlfriend," Amy spat. "And maybe I'm crazy, but that generally means we're totally honest with each other." She paused for a breath. Ty's eyes grew wide with hurt and surprise, but Amy went on. "But maybe you just didn't care enough to tell me. Maybe you figured since I'm leaving anyway, I didn't need to know. Isn't that the truth of it, Ty?"

Before he could answer, she turned and ran up the stairs.

Chapter Seven

❧

Amy refused to come downstairs the next day. She allowed Lou into her room to bring some breakfast and lunch, but apart from that she felt too miserable to see anyone. Soraya called her cell, but Amy couldn't bear to even rehash the details with her, so she didn't answer.

By the afternoon, she realized that the effects of the concussion had more or less gone. Her shoulder was still a little stiff, but her head didn't hurt anymore. She could stand up and walk across the room without feeling at all dizzy. Amy wished the ache in her heart could be cured so easily.

As the evening began to draw in, she stood at her bedroom window and looked down onto the garden. Nancy had transformed it into a blaze of color. It had never been like that when Marion was alive — apart from growing herbs for her remedies, Amy's mom had always been far too busy with the horses to give the flowers much attention. But gardening was Nancy's passion, and she had cultivated the shrubby, neglected borders into glorious flower beds.

It was just one thing that had changed in the last couple of years, and there were plenty more changes to come. Amy opened the window and felt the warm evening breeze on her face. The summer was flying by, and the accident made her feel as if she'd lost even more of it. In another month or so she would be leaving all this behind. She listened to the clop of a horse's hooves on the yard and her heart tightened in grief. She turned away and sat on her bed once more.

There was a knock on the door, and Lou peeked in. "Hi, there. Can I come in?" She was smiling.

Amy nodded, and Lou perched on the bed next to her. "I know I sound like a broken record, but how are you feeling?" she asked.

"My head feels fine today," Amy mumbled. "How's Sugarfoot?"

"Still pretty much the same, but Scott says we have to give it time," Lou said. She smiled. "You'll be able to check on him yourself soon. Listen, I was wondering if I could persuade you to come down to supper. Scott's coming over. We have some news."

Amy looked at her sister. She noticed that Lou's face

was glowing with happiness. In spite of herself, Amy was curious.

"Please. For me," Lou pleaded.

"OK," Amy conceded. "But if I don't feel well, I'll come back up."

"That's fine," Lou said. Impulsively, she leaned forward and gave Amy a hug. "Thank you."

❧

An hour later, Amy made her way downstairs feeling nervous. To her relief, Ty and Joni had gone home, leaving just Lou, Grandpa, Scott, and Nancy. Everyone seemed determined to behave as normally as possible around her, and the accident wasn't mentioned once, though Nancy did give her a quick hug. Nancy and Grandpa had cooked together and had made a special effort — a leg of lamb garnished with fresh rosemary from the garden, along with a salad of cherry tomatoes and cucumbers.

Everyone sat down while Grandpa placed the serving dishes on the table.

"I think Scott and I should make our announcement right away," said Lou, helping herself to some salad. "I don't think I can wait anymore."

"Oh, good," said Nancy. "We're all bursting with curiosity."

Amy nodded, realizing she was holding her breath.

She studied Lou and Scott's beaming faces. This was going to be good news. Amy felt a ray of hope pierce her gloomy mood.

"Scott and I are going to have a baby," Lou announced with a grin.

"Oh, my! Congratulations!" Nancy exclaimed. She kissed Lou on both cheeks. Grandpa stood up and walked around the table to hug his granddaughter, and Amy saw a tear in the corner of his eye. Despite her conflicted emotions, a bubble of happiness was swelling inside her. She was going to be an aunt! For an instant, she forgot all about her resentment toward Lou and gave her sister a big hug.

The rest of the evening was filled with happy chatter about the baby. Lou was convinced it would be a boy, while Scott felt certain it would be a girl.

"If it's a boy, we decided we'll name him Jack," Lou said, and Amy saw Grandpa tear up again.

"A great-grandfather," he murmured, shaking his head. "How come I don't feel that old?"

Nancy put her arm around his shoulder and gave him a squeeze. "Because you're not, Jack Bartlett," she said firmly, and everyone chuckled. Even Amy.

By the time Nancy served coffee — tea for Lou — Amy realized she was exhausted. Her head was feeling heavy again and she decided she ought to get some rest. She wished everyone good night and walked slowly upstairs, then lay in bed listening to the faint murmur of voices from downstairs. She grew drowsy and smiled to herself as she thought of Lou's news. It was almost surreal. Lou, pregnant! But then she felt a sudden twinge of sadness. *Mom would have been a grandma,* she reflected before drifting into sleep.

❧

Amy was woken the next morning by the rattle of a cup and saucer outside her door. "Amy, I've brought you a cup of tea," called Grandpa.

"Ohhh . . . come in," said Amy, sitting up. "What time is it?" she asked as Grandpa placed the tea by her bedside.

"Almost eight o'clock," Jack replied cheerily. "The day's well on its way."

Amy leaned back against her pillows and took a sip of tea. She felt as though she could have slept forever. She remembered the happy family meal the night before, but it seemed distant now, as though it had happened to someone else. She still couldn't believe Lou was going to be a mom.

"I just made a batch of muffins," Grandpa said. "I expect you'd like some before you get out on the yard."

Amy looked at him in surprise. The yard? Already?

Grandpa smiled and squeezed her arm, then stood up and headed for the door. "See you downstairs," he said.

Amy slid back down under the covers, feeling sleep creep up on her again. But she knew she shouldn't allow herself to drift off. Grandpa was right. She *was* ready to go back out on the yard. She'd been going stir-crazy, stuck indoors.

Amy showered and dressed. When she went downstairs Ty and Joni were sitting at the kitchen table. She avoided looking at either of them as Grandpa put a plate in front of her.

"How many muffins do you all want?" Jack asked.

"Two for me, please," Ty said, and Joni asked for one.

Jack placed a tray of hot blueberry muffins on the table. "Take as many as you like. There's plenty more where they came from."

Feeling self-conscious, Amy poured herself some orange juice and reached for a muffin, while Joni was reaching for the same one.

"Oh! Sorry," said Amy, dropping it hurriedly.

Joni flushed. "No, I'm sorry."

The two girls hesitated. Amy drew back her hand, so Joni smiled and put the muffin on her own plate.

"Do you want to walk around the yard after breakfast?" she asked after a moment of silence. "You know, so I can bring you up to date on all the horses."

She was genuinely trying to be friendly, Amy realized. She made herself nod, and she bit into her muffin, still painfully conscious of Ty's presence but unable to raise her eyes to his. The morning was going to be even more difficult than she'd imagined.

With breakfast over, Amy pulled on her yard boots, feeling increasingly anxious. Out there, on the yard, Fanfare waited. There would be no way to get around seeing him. She wished she had the courage to ask Joni how he had been doing since the accident, but she knew she couldn't bear to hear. The only way to know was to face him herself.

"So, where to first?" Joni asked brightly as they stepped outside. "Sugarfoot will be glad to see you. He's been so wobbly, poor thing. Scott's still worried about him."

Amy took a deep breath. "I need to see Fanfare," she said, surprising herself.

Joni looked surprised as well. "Oh! Of course. He's in the back barn."

They walked down the track side by side. The weather had cooled, and a fresh breeze was blowing. It was good to be outdoors again, but as they neared the barn, Amy found that her heart was pounding. What if the recent accident had deepened Fanfare's fears? And what if seeing her triggered them again? She stared at the big barn door.

"You go in," she said to Joni. "I'll join you in a minute."

Joni hesitated, then opened the door and stepped

inside. Amy realized that her palms were sweating, and she wiped them on her jeans. She closed her eyes and inhaled deeply to calm herself down. Then she walked in.

Joni was inside Fanfare's stall, stroking his neck and feeding him some horse cookies. She had left the half door open, and Amy approached slowly. The paint horse wasn't aware of her yet, and she didn't want to alarm him. She reached the door and Fanfare looked up.

The gelding instantly threw up his head and whinnied, knocking the cookies from Joni's hand.

"Hey, hey, steady," Joni said in a soothing tone. She smiled at Amy. "He's still a little jumpy."

He's more than that, Amy thought, swallowing. As she'd feared, Fanfare was reacting to her presence with suspicion and anxiety. Gathering all her courage, she took a step into the stall. Fanfare snorted, showing the whites of his eyes. Amy took another step and slowly raised her hand to stroke the horse's neck, noting as she did so that her fingers were shaking.

As soon as she touched his skin, the paint horse backed away, barging into Joni and ramming his haunches against the stall wall. Amy felt a cry of despair rising inside her. She clapped her hands to her mouth, devastated, and ran out of the stall. Fanfare's response couldn't have been worse. Why *should* the horse trust her? All she had done was compound Fanfare's trauma by taking him out on the road. Joni and Ty could handle him fine. She felt utterly useless. Blindly, she ran up to the yard and into the house.

She almost crashed into Lou, who was drinking a glass of milk in the kitchen. "Amy! What's wrong?"

Amy paused, drawing a breath. "You were right in the first place, Lou," she said in a strangled voice as the tears started to fall. "I wasn't equipped to know the truth about Fanfare. And I can't work with him now. It's too much . . . for . . . for both of us." She suppressed a sob. "Ty and Joni will have to help him on their own."

Then she turned and ran up the stairs to her bedroom, slamming the door shut. She flung herself facedown on the bed and wept into her pillow.

A few minutes later, she heard a knock.

"Amy. It's Ty. Can I talk to you?"

Amy sat up and stared at the door.

"Please. Just for a minute. We need to talk."

The image of Fanfare shying away from her tore into Amy's mind, and she buried her head in her hands. "There's nothing to talk about," she answered gruffly. "Just leave me alone."

There was silence outside the door. For a moment, she thought that Ty would come in anyway. But then she heard his footsteps going down the stairs, and she felt another, wilder stab of pain. She abandoned herself to it, crying and punching her pillow until she felt weak and exhausted.

❧

A couple of hours later, Amy felt calmer. She sat on her bed, wondering how she was going to get through the rest of the summer. It would be unbearable to spend time on the yard, but she couldn't spend the whole time in her room. Maybe she should give Soraya a call and go out with her and Matt. They could go shopping for clothes, and talk about college plans and posters for their dorm rooms. And it might be her last chance to spend some time with them before they all went their separate ways.

What about Ty? a voice whispered in Amy's head. *What about Spindle?* She stood up, trying to push the thoughts away. The less time she spent dwelling on Heartland, the easier it would be to leave.

She walked to her dressing table and picked up her hairbrush. Standing in front of the mirror, she brushed her long light-brown hair. Her nose was red from all the crying, and her gray eyes were puffy. *That's enough,* she told herself, and wiped away the last of her tears with a tissue.

Feeling thirsty, Amy decided to get herself a glass of lemonade before calling Soraya. She walked quietly

down the stairs, hoping the kitchen would be empty —
but it wasn't. She heard voices and stopped, trying to
figure out who was there. After a few moments, she
realized it was Lou, Ty, and two other people whose
voices she didn't recognize.

Curious, she stepped closer to the door, careful to stay
out of sight, and listened. She felt a jolt. She *did* recognize one of the voices — it was Mrs. Hughes, Kristin's
mother. And the other person was a girl, who sounded a
bit younger than Amy. It must be Kristin herself. Amy
crept closer to the door, holding her breath.

"It's going slowly," she heard Ty say. "But Joni's
working with him every day, and we're still confident he
can make a complete turnaround."

"Joni?" Kristin sounded puzzled. "I thought her name
was Amy."

There was a pause.

"You're thinking of my sister," said Lou. "But Joni's
doing most of the work with Fanfare at the moment."

"That's right, your sister," said Mrs. Hughes. "But
wasn't it Amy who . . . We thought . . ." She seemed to
be struggling to find the right words. "Scott explained
that you and Amy might have a special understanding of
a horse like Fanfare. Especially Amy."

Another pause. Amy held her breath, her heart thudding so loudly that she expected someone in the kitchen
would hear it and discover her at any moment.

"Well . . ." Lou began.

"He did say what had happened — he told us about . . . about your mother. I'm so sorry," said Mrs. Hughes in an emotional voice. "I don't know what I would have done if I'd lost John. As it is . . ." She trailed off.

There was the sound of Mrs. Hughes sniffing, and rummaging in a bag. Then Amy heard her blow her nose, and she felt her own throat tighten in sympathy.

"Is John any better?" Lou asked gently.

"Still no change at the moment," said Mrs. Hughes. "But Kristin's on the mend, aren't you, honey?" she added, sounding brighter.

"I think so," said Kristin. "My arm doesn't hurt so much now. The cast's really itchy, though."

The mood seemed to lighten with her remark, and Ty offered more tea or coffee.

"No, thank you, we should be going," said Mrs. Hughes. "You will let me know about Fanfare, won't you?"

"Of course," said Lou. "And I can assure you that Joni's the best person to be working with him at the moment."

Amy closed her eyes. She knew exactly what Lou thought. She'd known it for days now. But it didn't make it easier to hear it again, however true it might be.

"Well . . . I guess so," said Mrs. Hughes. "I'm sure you know best."

Amy heard the sound of chairs scraping back from the table. As the front door opened and everyone trooped outside, she let out her breath and went into the kitchen. She peered out the window to watch Mrs. Hughes and Kristin climb into their car, with Lou and Ty standing by to wave them off. Quickly, she grabbed some cookies from the jar and poured herself a glass of lemonade, then made for the stairs. But she heard them come back in.

"It's really for the best, Ty," Lou was saying.

"Look, Lou, I'm sorry, but I just don't agree," Ty replied. He sounded unusually heated, and Amy paused to listen. "I don't think Joni is the right person."

"Amy can't cope with Fanfare, Ty. Not after what happened."

Amy's mouth dropped open. They were talking about her again! Making decisions about her as if her own opinion didn't count.

"But Joni won't be able to get through to him like Amy could." Ty sounded angry and frustrated.

"Well, I think she can — and as a matter of fact, Amy thinks so, too," Lou said defensively. "She even said so this morning."

"You can't listen to Amy right now!" Ty exclaimed. "She's upset and temperamental. I know that if I talked to her —"

Amy couldn't stand it. She wasn't going to let them

decide her fate. Not Lou, not Ty, not anyone. She darted back to the kitchen door and threw it open.

"Ty, can't you just drop it?" she cried. Lou and Ty were facing each other across the kitchen table. They turned to face Amy in astonishment, guilt written across both their faces. "Lou's right. I *can't* handle Fanfare. Joni is doing just fine without me."

"Amy . . ." Lou began.

"You don't need to say anything," Amy declared, her voice trembling. She glared at them both, tears welling in her eyes. "I don't want anything more to do with that horse, OK? The sooner everyone accepts that, the better."

Chapter Eight

❧

"No!" The word exploded out of Ty, making both Amy and Lou start in surprise. "I won't accept it," he persisted. "You're the right person to treat Fanfare, Amy. The only person. I can't believe you don't see that."

Before Amy could respond, Lou moved around the table to place herself between Amy and Ty. "That's not for you to say, Ty," Lou said quietly but firmly.

"And why's that?" Ty demanded, his eyes flashing. Amy thought she had never seen him so angry.

Lou hesitated. "Because you don't fully understand . . ."

"What you and Amy went through after Marion's death? I was here, too, remember?" Ty gripped the back of a chair and stared at Lou. When he spoke again, it was more calmly, but with a steely determination. "Yes.

It's true. I can't relate to your and Amy's pain. But the fact is, I know Amy. She's stronger than you think. And *because* of her past experience — that's exactly why she'll be able to reach Fanfare."

"Ty, it's inappropriate for you to make this call," Lou said crisply.

Ty shook his head. "Lou, you know I have nothing but respect for you. But I think it was a mistake for you to keep Fanfare's history from Amy. And you're making another mistake now."

Amy listened to their exchange with mounting fury. Finally, she could no longer keep her frustration to herself.

"Stop it!" she cried, stepping closer to Ty. "Both of you, stop it! This is exactly what led to Fanfare's accident in the first place — everybody making decisions on my behalf." She cleared her throat and crossed her arms over her chest. "*I'm* making the decision here. And I don't want to work with Fanfare. In fact, I'd really just like to focus on preparing for college — "

Instead of backing away, Ty stepped closer to Amy too, until they were directly facing each other.

"This isn't right. You're running away from this problem, and you know it." Ty's stare was penetrating. Amy was speechless. In all her years of knowing him, she'd never seen Ty this impassioned, this resolute. His expression was stubborn. He was not giving up.

"You can't turn your back on Fanfare!" Ty went on.

"He needs you. You're the one who can understand his pain. Not Joni. Think about it."

"I don't *want* to! I've thought about it enough!" Amy cried.

"No, you haven't. You've just been sitting in your room thinking about your own grief." Ty's gaze remained steady, challenging her, and Amy took a step back. She hated to admit it, but Ty was right.

"Don't do this, Amy," he added softly. "Don't sit on the sidelines. It's not you. And it's not what Marion taught you to do."

That was the final straw. Amy turned and tore up the stairs, her heart bursting. She ran into her bedroom and slammed the door, feeling the vibration echo through the house. How could he? How could he bring up Marion again when he knew how fragile Amy was feeling? She grabbed a pillow and thumped it, too angry to cry. The image of Ty's green eyes blazed through her mind. Amy was furious at him, but a tiny part of her also felt grateful. Ty's fierce words had shaken her out of her stupor. She'd rather be angry than sorrowful. For the first time in days, she felt energetic, as if she wanted to do something active and productive. But what?

Ty's words echoed in her head. *He needs you. You're running away from this problem.* She buried her face in her hands. She *wasn't* running away. Or was she?

🙞

After Amy had calmed down, she went into Marion's room. It had been kept just as her mother had left it, and Amy rarely visited there now. But she made herself sit in the faded, rose-patterned armchair in the corner and remember the weeks that had followed the accident. Spartan had come to Heartland when both he and Amy had recovered physically — Amy in the hospital, Spartan in Scott's clinic — and all they had to show they'd been in the accident were their scars. But their emotions, the scars hidden underneath the skin, had been another matter entirely. The beautiful bay horse had been full of pain and anger. He had turned his fury on Amy as though he blamed her for what had happened, and he had lashed out at her time and time again.

And somehow, despite the depths of her own despair, she had made it through. She had believed that Spartan could overcome his trauma, and she had helped him do it. She remembered something Scott had said at the time: *You'll be able to cope with him, Amy. If anyone can, you can.* And she had believed him. She had stood up to the horse's anger and forced him to accept her. And by accepting her, he had accepted his own terrible experience and found the strength to move on.

Join up. That was how she had reached him. In a

torrential storm, Amy had taken Spartan down to the
training ring and battled with him in the thunder and
pouring rain, driving him away from her. She had lost all
sense of time as Spartan had galloped on and on, around
and around the ring. But at last he had decided to fight no
longer. Amy still recalled that remarkable moment when
he had joined her in the center of the ring. She remembered every detail. In that moment, Amy had made peace
not only with Spartan — but also with herself.

Amy stood up and wandered over to Marion's book-
shelf, looking at all the books on horses and healing.
Books on finding one's inner strength. Her mother hadn't
had an easy life — there had been the accident that had
forced her husband to stop riding, and the subsequent
divorce. But Marion never ran away from anything.
Marion had faced up to her own losses and difficulties
and turned them into something beautiful — her work at
Heartland. The work that lived on in the people she had
left behind. Ty was right. Marion never sat on the sidelines, and she would *never* have wanted Amy to, either. Amy
choked up as she ran her finger down the spine of a book.
Marion would have wanted her to work with Fanfare.

Amy returned to her room, changed into her yard
clothes, and pulled her hair back into a ponytail. She could
do this. She *had* to do this. There was no other way to come
to grips with her memories. Amy took a deep breath.
When she was ready, she looked out the window. The

afternoon was hot and still, and dusk was just beginning to fall. She heard a car door slam and guessed it was Joni or Ty heading off for the evening. She slipped quietly downstairs, out through the back door, and around the garden onto the yard.

The yard was deserted. Amy took a lead rope from the tack room and turned on the floodlights in the training ring, then hurried down to the back barn and let herself in. Fanfare had his back to her. The orange bulb in his stall lit up the white patches in his coat, bathing him in a fiery glow. Amy approached slowly, holding her breath, and unbolted the half door.

Fanfare turned. The instant he saw her, he laid his ears back and rolled the whites of his eyes. Amy's first instinct was to walk away again, but she forced herself to stay, Ty's words from earlier ringing in her head.

"Hello there, Fanfare," Amy said in a low, calm voice. "Looks like you and I have some work to do."

The paint horse's muscles were tense. Amy stepped toward him, but he raised his head and snorted, backing away from her. She reached out her hand for his halter and he plunged past her to the other side of the stall, knocking over his water bucket and cannoning against the half door.

"Steady, steady," Amy said, feeling the wrench of his rejection. She'd faced nervous horses before, but this seemed so much more personal, as if Fanfare were able to read her self-doubt.

She stood quietly for a moment, waiting for the gelding's panic to subside. His neck was glistening with sweat, and Amy's heart contracted, thinking of how relaxed and obedient he had appeared before their accident. His trauma had been buried deep inside, but now it was out on the surface, raw and plain to see. Amy felt a stab of sympathy. Ty had been right about that, too. She *could* relate exactly to how Fanfare was feeling.

She moved toward the horse again. Once more he veered away, but this time she was ready and lunged for his halter. Fanfare tossed his head and pulled backward, his muscles taut with fear. Amy clung on, struggling with the lead rope until she managed to secure the clip. Then she stepped back in relief.

The gelding fought her all the way to the training ring, crabbing sideways and resisting the pull of the rope. Amy gritted her teeth. She couldn't give in. She and Fanfare were going to get through this together.

At last they made it to the ring, and Amy pushed the gate open. Sensing freedom, Fanfare pushed past her, almost sending her flying. She stumbled forward, clutching the lead rope. The powerful horse dragged her out into the center of the ring, his head held high and his nostrils flaring.

Regaining her balance, Amy caught up with him and unclipped the rope from his halter. "Go on! Go!" she shouted, waving her arms at him. "Get away from me!"

With a shrill whinny of distress, Fanfare bucked and cantered off around the floodlit ring. The air was thick with moisture, and rain threatened. Suddenly, Amy felt as if she were back in the ring with Spartan. She ran after Fanfare, her heart ablaze.

"Go!" she hollered at him again and again as he careened around the ring.

The paint horse put his head between his legs and bucked, as though trying to fling off his agony, but there was no escape from it. He barged up to the fence, hunting for a way out and finding none. He was trapped in the ring with Amy, the person who reminded him of his encounter with the truck and his terrifying experience in the horse trailer. Around and around he galloped, his eyes wild with fear and his sides heaving, while Amy drove him on, shouting furiously to make sure he didn't stop.

She wasn't sure how long she ran, flapping her arms and keeping the horse on the move. Her cheeks flamed scarlet in the warm, still air, and she was drenched in sweat. But she never took her eyes off Fanfare. She bored into him with her gaze, daring him to remain in the frightening, lonely track at the edges of the ring. She knew it was a difficult choice — either to stay where he was or to give in and put his trust in the person who had let him down.

Gasping for breath, she wondered if he was ever going

to respond. Then, at last, she saw the signs she was hoping for. Fanfare twisted his ear toward her, lowering his neck in submission. His pace slowed. As she had done with Spartan, Amy drew on her last reserves of energy to drive him away again, wanting to be absolutely sure of his surrender. He cantered off, but his stride lacked conviction. His coat glistened with sweat, and the next time he lowered his head he began to make chewing motions with his lips, begging Amy to let him stop. Letting out a long breath, Amy dropped her shoulders and slowly turned her back on the paint horse.

It didn't take long. Fanfare stood for a moment, his breath coming in noisy rasps. Then Amy heard his soft footfalls walking toward her across the ring. Blowing through his nose, the gelding touched her shoulder with his muzzle and gently lipped at her hair.

Amy couldn't believe it. She didn't think she'd ever get through to Fanfare. A great wave of joy rose up in her. She turned and stroked Fanfare's neck, gazing into his soft brown eyes. He showed no sign of resistance. Amy hugged him, the relief so strong that it made her feel weak. Now she understood why Ty had behaved as he did that morning. Just as Ty had forced her to choose to come down here and face her demons, this horse had made a choice, too — and he had chosen to trust Amy completely.

Chapter Nine

❧

As Amy stroked Fanfare's nose, leaning her face against his cheek, the paint horse suddenly turned to the gate with his ears pricked. Amy followed his gaze. She was astonished to see a figure emerging from the shadows near the path. For a moment she felt a cold jab of fear to think that a stranger might be wandering around Heartland at night. But then he stepped under the first floodlight, and Amy saw who it was.

Ty.

He opened the gate and walked toward her, smiling softly.

"I — I thought you went home," Amy stuttered. The memory of their encounter made her feel almost shy around him.

Ty stopped a few yards away from her and shook his head. "I was guessing you'd come down here with Fanfare sooner or later," he told her. "I didn't want to miss it, so I hung around. I hope you don't mind."

Amy's heart leaped. "So you saw everything?"

Ty nodded.

Amy met his gaze. Slowly, she dropped Fanfare's lead rope on the ground and stepped toward Ty. He opened his arms and she rushed into them. He wrapped her in a warm hug.

"I'm so proud of you," he whispered into her hair. "Please don't ever doubt yourself again, OK?"

Amy leaned against Ty's chest, unable to speak for happiness. Being so close to him again made her realize how deeply she had missed him. They stood for several moments in silence, holding each other, and only looked up when Fanfare approached, his expression puzzled, to blow into Amy's hair. She turned, laughing, and hugged the paint horse again.

"Are we neglecting you, Fanfare?" she teased as the horse nuzzled her shoulder. His coat was still streaked with sweat from galloping around the ring, so Amy picked up the lead rope and clipped it onto his halter. "We should give you a rubdown before your muscles get cold."

With Ty beside her, she led Fanfare through the gate and up the path to the barn. Ty went to get a grooming kit while she settled the paint horse into his stall. Fanfare still wanted nothing more than to be close to Amy, constantly butting her with his nose, and she stroked his forelock. Join up always moved her in some way, but this particular join up had been especially meaningful. Only this morning Amy had felt certain that Fanfare would never trust her again. Now they shared a special understanding.

Ty soon returned and they set to work on either side of the horse with body brushes, working in broad sweeps along the main muscles.

After a while, Ty paused and looked at Amy across Fanfare's back. "I never got a chance to apologize," he said quietly.

Amy shook her head. "Ty . . ."

Ty cleared his throat, his eyes serious. "No, Amy, let me. I'm so sorry I didn't come to you with the truth about Fanfare. I was wrong. We all were. I think you proved that tonight." Ty stopped brushing for a minute. "And I'm sorry for the way I acted this morning. I just felt like there was no other way . . ."

Amy nodded. "I *needed* you to push me like you did this morning, Ty. Sure, I was upset at the time. But of course I understand that you were doing it because you cared about me. And Fanfare."

"I care about you more than you know, Amy," Ty murmured, his eyes on her face.

Amy bit her lip, overwhelmed by emotion. "And yes, it was hard for me to accept that everyone knew about Fanfare but me. Lou was just being overprotective, and I can understand why. But I was upset for other reasons. I guess I've been feeling left out lately."

"Because you're leaving." It was a statement, not a question.

Amy nodded. Ty could always get to the heart of the matter.

Ty stepped around Fanfare and stroked Amy's hair as she laid her head against his chest. "I wish you *weren't* leaving," he said eventually.

Amy's heart almost stopped. "You — you don't want me to go?" she managed to ask.

"Of course I don't." Ty's voice cracked. "But I still think it's the right thing for you to do. And you'll be close by. I'll come visit, and you'll have vacations, and summers . . . this isn't good-bye."

Amy searched his face again as they stepped apart, their hands still linked.

"The thing is," Ty continued thoughtfully, "Heartland will always be here. And Heartland will always need you. You shouldn't ever feel left out. You don't even realize how much we all depend on you."

"Really?" Amy whispered.

Ty gripped her hands and gazed into her eyes.

"Of course," he said intensely. "Think about the horses you've helped over the years. Spartan and Flint and Gallant Prince. Molly, Venture, Mercury — so many. And now Fanfare. Heartland wouldn't be what it is today without you."

Amy smiled. "And *I* couldn't have done any of it without you," she replied truthfully. "Thank you," she whispered. "Thank you for everything."

Fanfare turned to look at them curiously, as though he wondered why they had stopped work. His eyes were calm and bright, with no trace of nervousness, and Amy reached up to stroke his neck.

"And we still have the rest of the summer," Ty reminded her with a grin. "You're not gone just yet."

Amy nodded. "You're right," she said, putting her arms around his neck. "From now on, I'll be here one hundred percent until I have to leave in August."

❧

They finished Fanfare's rubdown in companionable silence. By the time they left, the gelding was pulling at his hay net, and Amy gave him one final pat before stepping out of his stall. She walked out into the still summer air and breathed in deeply. Ty was right — they still had plenty of time, and there was a lot to catch up on from the past week.

"I'd like to see Spindle," she said to Ty as they walked up to the tack room with the grooming kit. "I've missed that little guy so much. And Sugarfoot. How is he?"

Ty's face fell. "Sugarfoot's not great," he told her. "I haven't wanted to worry Lou, but I don't think the medication's working very fast, if at all."

"Are you sure?" Amy felt dismayed. Lou had seemed so positive over the last few days.

Ty hesitated. "If you ask me, he's been getting worse," he admitted, placing the kit on the shelf. "Want to go and see him?"

Amy nodded, and they walked across the front yard to the little Shetland's stall. Ty quietly unbolted the half door and they went in. Sugarfoot was lying down, his head resting on his bedding, but he struggled to his feet as they entered. Amy was appalled. Standing was clearly much more of an effort for him than when she had first noticed the problem, out in the pasture. Sugarfoot stood with his legs splayed wide for balance, sweat breaking out along his flanks.

"Hello, boy," Amy murmured, caressing the pony's thick furry ears and running her hand along his back. He had clearly lost weight, and she could feel his spine beneath his coat. "You're feeling a bit under the weather, aren't you?" She turned to Ty. "What does Scott say?"

"He's not too optimistic," he replied. "He put Sugarfoot on anti-inflammatory drugs because his symptoms have gotten worse. The problem is that the drugs will kill the protozoa, but the damage to the central nervous system can be irreversible." He glanced down, his face coloring. "It's pretty serious, Amy. But Scott doesn't want Lou to know the full story. Especially now that she's pregnant."

Amy stared at Ty. She could understand how Scott felt. Lou was deeply affected by Sugarfoot. But Amy also knew too well how Lou would feel if she discovered that people were hiding the truth from her. Amy couldn't let her feel left out, as she had been.

"I'll talk to Lou tomorrow," she said. "She needs to know. Don't you think?"

Ty looked relieved. "After everything that happened last week?" he asked. "Yes. Honesty is always the best way, even if you're just trying to protect the people you love."

Amy examined Sugarfoot more closely, feeling the muscle wastage in his hindquarters. He shifted uneasily when she applied pressure to his back, and she realized that he was in pain. "Poor Sugarfoot," she murmured, her mind running through the remedies and herbs that might help when paired with Scott's conventional treatments. She had to do more research. She looked at Ty. "Tomorrow I'm going to find out everything I can about this disease," she declared. "And I promise you that we're going to beat it."

❧

They left the Shetland to rest for the night and stepped back out onto the yard. Ty fished out the keys to his pickup. "You should go visit Spindle on your own," he said. "I don't want to get in the way," he added with a teasing smile.

Amy grinned. "If you insist," she said. It was wonderful to be joking with Ty again, as if everything was back to normal. "I'll see you in the morning."

Ty gave her one last hug. "I'll never forget seeing you join up with Fanfare," he spoke into her ear. "You're stronger than you will ever realize, Amy."

"Only as strong as the person who made me do it," she responded, smiling up at him.

They kissed, and Amy watched Ty climb into the pickup and start the engine. Once she had waved him off, she walked back down toward the pastures in the warm night air. As she approached, she could hear the sound of horses cropping grass, and she whistled softly.

"Spindle!"

The horses were bunched together near the gate, and all raised their heads at the sound of her voice. At first she couldn't pick out the two-year-old among the shadows, but then she spotted his long, elegant legs and called again.

This time he snorted and turned toward the gate, his tail held high.

"So you haven't forgotten me," Amy murmured as Spindle stretched his muzzle toward her, wide-eyed in the moonlight. He whickered and accepted the mint that she found at the bottom of her pocket. Amy thought back to the other time she had left him — when she and Ty had gone away to see a friend in the Appalachian Mountains the year before. She had been worried then, too, that the colt might forget her. But he hadn't. As she played with Spindle's tufty forelock, Amy realized that close bonds were not so easily broken. Spindle's gentle, trusting nature meant that he would respond to many people, yet still feel closest to her. Whoever worked with him when she had gone and whatever happened while she was away, Spindle would always be there.

❧

The next morning, Amy got up at her usual early hour. Her headache had more or less gone, and apart from the soreness in her muscles from chasing after Fanfare, she felt fine. It was time once again to tackle her share of the chores on the yard, and Amy realized how much she was looking forward to it. She went down onto the yard and found that neither Ty nor Joni had arrived yet, so she walked straight across to Sugarfoot's stall.

There was little change from the night before. The Shetland had eaten half his hay and seemed reasonably comfortable. Amy reflected that at least EPM seemed slow-moving and reminded herself of her resolution to do some research and speak to Lou. Then she collected a wheelbarrow and went to the back barn to start mucking out.

Outside the barn, she hesitated, thinking of Fanfare. How would the horse react to her today? What if the join up hadn't left its mark, and he shied away from her? She couldn't bear that — it would be just too painful to start all over again. She closed her eyes and thought of Spartan. He hadn't rejected her once they had been through join up. There was no reason for Fanfare to do so, either. Taking a deep breath, she pushed open the door and stepped inside.

Fanfare was pulling the last mouthfuls of hay from his hay net but turned his head at the sound of the barn door.

"Fanfare," Amy called in a voice that was barely above a whisper.

The paint horse stood still, a wisp of hay dangling from his mouth, and Amy could feel her heart beating faster. Fanfare's ears pricked forward, and he gave a whicker from somewhere deep inside his throat. He was welcoming her.

Amy felt almost weak with relief. She put the wheelbarrow down and walked to the horse's half door.

Fanfare put his head over it and she gave him a handful of horse cookies before rubbing his nose playfully.

She was just about to start the mucking out when she heard footsteps outside the barn door. The door opened and Joni walked in.

"Oh!" she exclaimed, startled. "Hi, Amy."

Amy flushed and smiled awkwardly. She hadn't seen Joni since her terrible encounter with Fanfare in the barn. Amy realized that it must be a surprise for Joni to see her standing there bonding with the paint horse. "Hi," she responded. She nodded toward the wheelbarrow. "I'm fine with mucking out today."

Joni looked from Amy to Fanfare and back again, clearly curious. "Would you like some help?"

"I think I can manage," said Amy. "I'm feeling a lot better now."

"That's great," said Joni, her voice warm. "It's good to see you up and about again."

Amy could tell that she meant it. Joni really didn't have a problem about sharing responsibilities on the yard, Amy realized. She was just trying to be helpful. Amy was ashamed to finally grasp that all the tension between her and Joni had come from *her* own insecurities about leaving Heartland.

"Thanks. It's good to be back," Amy replied.

Joni flashed her a smile and headed for the barn door.

"Joni?" Amy called after her.

She turned around, her expression curious.

"I just wanted to say that I — I know the whole story now," Amy said, reaching up to stroke Fanfare's neck. "Thanks for trying to warn me about riding out. I'm sorry I snapped at you."

Embarrassment showed briefly in Joni's clear blue eyes. "No, it makes sense that you were frustrated. I hope you're not upset that . . ."

"I've gotten past it," Amy cut in. "And I joined up with Fanfare last night. I think we kind of understand each other now."

Joni looked relieved. "Well, I'm glad someone understands him," she said. "I was doing my best, but I didn't feel I was reaching him at all."

"I guess I know what he's been through," said Amy. "He's a difficult one to read."

Joni nodded. "You're the right person to handle him, Amy. That's what Ty said all along, and I agree with him." She smiled again and opened the barn door. "Good luck. And welcome back. It wasn't the same without you."

🙢

Amy finished mucking out the barn and went to the front yard. Lou's car was in the driveway, and Amy caught a glimpse of her sister's blond head in Sugarfoot's stall. She hesitated. She hadn't talked to her sister since the big argument with Ty in the kitchen. And Amy felt as if she still hadn't completely resolved the Fanfare issue with Lou. Amy wondered what they had said to each other after she had gone. *It doesn't matter,* she told herself. *Sugarfoot is what matters now.* She walked across the yard and looked over the half door.

"Hi, Lou," she said quietly.

Lou was giving Sugarfoot a bran mash and looked up, clearly surprised to see her. "Amy! Are you working today?"

"I'm trying to get back into the routine. I think it's about time." Amy let herself into the Shetland's stall and watched as Sugarfoot nosed at the mash. "Ty was right, Lou. I had to face up to dealing with Fanfare."

Lou searched Amy's face, looking anxious.

"I joined up with him last night," Amy added, and she saw the shock on her sister's face. "It wasn't easy, but I think it's started the healing process for both of us."

Lou swallowed, then gave a small smile. She seemed at a loss about what to say. "I'm glad," she said eventually.

"Thank you for trying to protect me," said Amy. "I know that's all you were trying to do."

Lou nodded, biting her lip. "I'm sorry, Amy."

"I know I seemed really upset. And I was. But I understand now. I really do." Amy stroked Sugarfoot's forelock, and the little Shetland shifted uncomfortably. She caught the look of concern in Lou's eye. "He's not doing too well, is he?"

Lou shrugged. "Scott keeps saying the medication should work," she said. "But it doesn't seem to be kicking in yet."

Amy took a deep breath. "Lou, Scott really loves you, so he's trying to keep you from getting too anxious, but I think the situation is worse than it seems."

Lou looked sharply at Amy. "How do you know that?"

"Last night, Ty told me that Scott wasn't optimistic about Sugarfoot," Amy whispered.

For an instant, Lou looked stricken, her hand moving instinctively to rest on her still-flat belly, and Amy felt suddenly concerned. Maybe Scott was right to try not to alarm Lou. But then Amy thought of all the difficult times she and her sister had been through. Lou was strong whenever she needed to be. "I thought you should know," Amy added.

Lou reached down to touch Sugarfoot's neck and stroked it slowly. "Now you're the one to tell me the truth," she said with a wry smile, playing with the Shetland's mane. "I'm glad you did."

Amy watched her sister carefully. It was obvious that the irony of the situation hadn't escaped her. But it was also clear that Lou was saddened by Sugarfoot's condition.

"I guess he still has a good chance," Amy said gently. "I'm going to look up some information on the Internet this morning. Maybe there are things we can do to improve his chances."

Lou looked up. "That's a good idea."

Impulsively, Amy gave her sister a hug. "We'll get him better, Lou. We've done it before. *You've* done it before."

"Poor Sugarfoot," murmured Lou, her voice breaking. "You're right, Amy. We've got to fight for him with everything we've got."

Chapter Ten

❧

Once the chores were done, Amy spent the rest of the morning indoors, searching online for information about EPM. It soon became clear that Scott's treatment had followed the textbooks to the letter — antiprotozoan drugs, followed up with anti-inflammatories.

EPM seemed to be an odd disease with many mysteries surrounding it. Scientists thought that a horse could be a carrier for several years before developing any symptoms; some horses developed it quickly, some slowly, and many never at all. One of the factors that could affect its development was shock, or disruption of any kind. Amy frowned. Sugarfoot hadn't experienced any shocks. But there were other factors that might have played a part in its appearance, such as the number of protozoa that had been ingested in the first place, and which parts of the body they had managed to reach.

Amy read more about the illness and discovered to her relief that it was common for symptoms to worsen once treatment had been started. It would just take the pony a while to adjust. She also read that vitamin E supplements were thought to help, along with folic acid. Amy smiled as she realized that she had been helping his treatment from the outset with the remedies she had instinctively reached for at first.

As she sat thinking, it occurred to her that, generally, stress lowered the body's resistance to disease. Perhaps the reverse was true. If she could make Sugarfoot feel really happy and comfortable, he might fight off the infection naturally and tip the balance in his own favor. Feeling inspired, she went to the feed room and looked up her mom's notes on herbal remedies. Anything that would boost the immune system was worth trying, along with remedies that would lift Sugarfoot's spirits. She read that astralagus and echinacea both did wonders for the immune system, and that ginseng gave energy to convalescents. Gorse and gentian flower remedies would have an uplifting, positive effect, too. And, of course, she must tell Lou to sing to him, as she had done after Mrs. Bell died. Excited by her findings, Amy went in search of her sister.

Lou listened carefully when Amy found her in the

den. "It definitely makes sense," she agreed after Amy had finished. "Let's go for it. I'm willing to try anything, and Sugarfoot *has* to get better. I just wouldn't be able to bear it if he didn't."

Amy nodded. "Well, I'll deal with all the additional treatments," she said. "But I'll leave the singing to you."

Lou smiled. "You know, it felt awful to hear the truth this morning. But I understand why Scott didn't tell me. And I'm grateful to you. I guess that's how you felt about Fanfare."

"Exactly." Amy smiled. "Ty said something last night that kind of stuck in my mind. He said that I am stronger than I'll ever realize. Maybe that goes for both of us."

Lou's blue eyes filled with tears for a moment, but she blinked them away. "We've had to be," she said. "But I think we'll just keep on getting stronger." Her hand strayed to her stomach again. "After all, I've got this little one to be strong for now, too."

❧

Later that day, Amy went down to the pasture to catch Spindleberry. She was really looking forward to working with the two-year-old again, and she hummed a tune as she walked down the track. At the gate, she bumped into Joni, who was just returning from turning out Attitude. Amy asked after the spirited gelding, and Joni explained that he was finally making progress through a lot of firm handling and hard work.

"We think he was bored, basically," she finished. "Are you going to work with Spindle now?"

Amy nodded. "I thought I'd give him a session on the lunge. I guess you and Ty have been working him the past week."

"Actually, Ty's been lunging him on his own," said Joni.

Amy flushed. Of course. Amy remembered their earlier clash over Spindle, and she felt ashamed of the way she'd behaved.

"Well, how about giving me a hand now?"

Joni looked surprised and pleased. "Are you sure?"

"Absolutely," Amy responded. "After all, you'll be working with him a lot after I've left for school."

Joni smiled. "Well, that would be great," she said. "I'll wait here while you catch him."

Amy entered the pasture and called Spindle's name. He was grazing near the far fence but looked up at the sound of her voice. She called again, and he began to amble toward her, still chewing his last mouthful of grass.

"Good boy," she praised him, slipping the halter over his ears. "Ready for some work?"

In the training ring, Amy fitted the two-year-old with the lunging cavesson and sent him off around the ring with Joni at his head. It was soon obvious that he didn't really need Joni there. Ty had done a good job with him over the past few days, and he was pretty much used to working on his own. So Joni went to watch from the fence while Amy asked Spindle to walk and trot, and the pony obeyed willingly, forming a perfect circle as she nudged him on with the whip.

"I think you should take over," Amy called to Joni when the horse had completed a few circles in trot. "He needs to change the rein now anyway."

Joni's face split into a wide grin. She took the lunge line and whip and positioned herself where Amy had been standing. "Walk on!" she called as Amy hoisted herself onto the fence to watch.

Spindle stood still, staring at Amy. She sat motionless, not wanting to interfere, and willing the young horse to obey his new trainer. Joni stayed calm and tapped his haunches with the long lunging whip. Amy knew Joni had a lot of experience in lunging horses, and Amy was confident she would know exactly what to do. "Walk on!" she repeated in a firmer tone.

This time, Spindle responded, but he still seemed puzzled and his walk was little more than a dawdle.

"Push him on," Amy muttered to herself. She didn't want him thinking that he could get away with dragging his feet like that.

Joni wasn't happy, either. She clicked her tongue and nudged the bay gelding again, forcing him to listen to her.

Spindle shook his mane and walked on with a little more verve. With another nudge, he looked much more purposeful, and by the time Joni ordered him to trot, he had gotten the message — the person in the center was the one in control. He trotted on obediently, arching his neck, and Amy was surprised by how relieved she felt. She no longer felt possessive, just proud of both Spindle and Joni.

"That was great," she called, jumping off the fence as Joni brought the two-year-old back to a walk. "I think that's enough for today — he's still too young to do much. But you did a terrific job."

Joni shook her head, blushing. "It's thanks to you," she said, her blue eyes shining. "I know how much you love him, Amy. It can't be easy to hand over his training to someone else."

Amy smiled sadly. "It's not easy," she admitted. "But I know that he'll be in good hands with you and Ty. That's the important thing."

They led Spindle out of the ring and up toward the front yard. He was still full of energy, and Amy laughed as he jostled her playfully. "He needs to calm down a little," she said. "Why don't you give him a rubdown? I want to get some remedies ready for Sugarfoot."

"Sure," said Joni. "What remedies are you going to try?"

Amy explained the approach they were going to take with the Shetland, and Joni nodded understandingly.

"My mom does that kind of thing," she said. "She uses her veterinary knowledge to reach a diagnosis, then she backs up the conventional treatments with alternative therapies, like acupuncture."

"I guess that's how I'd like to work myself, in the long run," Amy said, suddenly feeling genuinely excited about the future. "But I have to get through college and vet school first!"

"I'm not worried about you," Joni said warmly. "You'll make a great vet, Amy. Anyone can see that."

❧

Joni's words were warming, but as Amy was hunting through the rows of brown bottles in the feed room, doubt began to prick at her again. Heartland was her whole life. Joining up with Fanfare had shown her that more deeply than any other experience. The memory of standing with Ty in the training ring swam before her. *I wish you weren't leaving. . . .*

Lou's voice broke into her thoughts. "Amy! Soraya's on the phone for you."

Amy made a note of the remedies she had reviewed so far and hurried onto the yard and into the farmhouse.

"Hi, Soraya," she said, picking up the phone.

"How are you doing?" Soraya asked immediately. "Are you feeling better? Matt and I have been really worried."

"I'm a lot better, thanks," said Amy. "Back in the barn, actually!" It felt so good to say those words.

"Wow," said Soraya. "That's amazing, Amy. Nothing seems to keep you down for long."

Amy laughed, thinking of the dark days she'd spent in her room. "Well, I'm not so sure about that," she said wryly. "But I guess I come around eventually."

"Of course you do," Soraya assured her. "And I'm glad. Especially since I have some good news."

"About what?"

"The party," her friend replied happily. "I haven't sent out the invitations yet, but I've made some calls just to check that people can make it. Amy, it's going to be great! *Everyone* can come."

"Who's everyone?" Amy asked with a smile. Soraya's exuberance about social activities may have annoyed her earlier in the summer, but now Amy felt nothing but fondness toward her loyal friend.

"Well, you and Ty and everyone at Heartland, naturally. And I knew you'd want people from Nick Halliwell's stables to be there, so I invited Ben and Daniel and . . . that other girl. Ben's girlfriend."

"Tara?"

"Oh, right." Soraya sounded breezy, but Amy knew that inviting Tara couldn't have been easy. For a long time, Soraya had harbored a crush on Ben, and it was only since she'd started going out with Matt that she'd gotten over her regret that they hadn't ever dated.

"Sounds great," said Amy. "Thanks, Soraya."

"You might not thank me when you find out who else I invited." Soraya chuckled. "I went through the list of everyone in our year and I felt I had to include . . ."

"Ashley." It was more of a statement than a question. Amy could guess the way Soraya's mind had been working. Snobby Ashley Grant had made things difficult for both Amy and Soraya at times. She and Amy were rivals when it came to riding, and Soraya was bitter toward her because Ashley had gone out with Matt. But Amy knew that Soraya didn't like to hold grudges. She probably wanted to get some closure with Ashley before they all headed off to college.

"You guessed it!"

Amy laughed. "Well, I can't say I'm thrilled. But that's big of you, Soraya. Really. So, should we get together so I can help you with the planning?"

"That'd be fantastic," Soraya enthused. "Are you sure you have time?"

"Of course. How about next week? I guess you need to choose music and decide on the food and all that kind of stuff." Amy found she was excited by the prospect.

"I know! It's only three and a half weeks from now. I'd better get my act together with those invitations!"

After they had said good-bye, Amy put the phone

down with a strange pang. *Three and a half weeks.* After Soraya's party, the summer would be almost over. And Amy would be on the brink of her new life. She frowned. Going away still didn't seem quite real. And somewhere in the back of her mind, a little voice whispered that maybe it wouldn't have to be.

∾

The summer days began to slip by. Amy made Fanfare and Spindle her priorities but helped with the other horses whenever she had time. Now that she had picked out the extra treatments for Sugarfoot, she left the care of the Shetland mainly to Lou and often heard the sound of her sister's sweet singing voice drifting across the yard. Lou remained calm and determined, and Amy hoped with all her heart that the little pony would pull through.

With each day, Fanfare seemed to let down his barriers more and more. He greeted Amy eagerly in the morning and seemed happy to be taken out to the training ring to work. Amy began to see just how affectionate the paint horse could be — and how willing to please his rider. She continued to work with him in the school but also led him around the yard and slowly introduced him to the vehicles parked in the driveway. Once he seemed comfortable with cars that were stationary, Amy got Ty to start the engine of his pickup. Fanfare's trust in Amy was remarkable. He was still nervous, but with her beside him, he barely flinched as she led him past the revving pickup.

Then, about ten days after first joining up with him, Amy was leading Fanfare back down to the barn when she saw a blue car coming up the driveway. It stopped outside the farmhouse. An unfamiliar figure climbed out of the passenger seat, and Amy's heart leaped. The slender girl with her arm in a cast could be only one person: Kristin Hughes.

Fanfare spotted Kristin at the same instant. He stood stock-still, his muscles trembling. Then he gave a trumpeting whinny, and Kristin turned to look.

"Fanfare!" The girl's joy at seeing her horse showed clearly on her face. She waved and made her way over.

Kristin was petite, with fine features and rich auburn hair cropped close to her head. Amy's immediate thought was that the girl seemed too slight for the big paint horse, but as she jogged toward them, Amy noticed that she was also wiry and in very fit shape, even after several weeks without riding. Kristin reached to hug the horse with her good arm, hiding the arm in the white cast behind her back.

Amy handed her the lead rope. "Hi, there. You must be Kristin. I'm Amy, Lou's sister."

Kristin turned from Fanfare to regard Amy curiously.

"Amy. It's good to meet you. But I thought Joni was working with Fanfare now."

"She was, and she did good work with him," Amy said. "But I took over about ten days ago."

"And how's he doing?" Kristin studied Fanfare carefully. "He seems much better."

Amy felt a rush of pleasure. She was glad that Kristin was so perceptive about her horse. "He's been coming along really well."

Kristin patted the paint horse happily. "I'm so relieved," she said, her voice choked with emotion. "It's been such a horrible time."

"I know," said Amy quietly. "I understand."

Kristin's solemn hazel eyes met hers for a moment. "Yes," she said. "I know you do. I — I'm sorry about what you went through."

They stood in silence for a moment, regarding each other. Somehow no more needed to be said. Both girls understood the effects of their harsh experiences without needing to express them in words.

Amy smiled as Mrs. Hughes approached them with Lou by her side. Fanfare recognized the woman, too, and snorted a welcome as she offered him a mint.

"Hello, Fanfare," said Mrs. Hughes. She shook Amy's hand. "Nice to see you, Amy. Lou tells me he's been making great strides with your help."

"He's getting there," said Amy. "He's been much more relaxed over the past week."

"Well, it's good news all around, then," said Mrs. Hughes. "We've just heard that John might make a full recovery after all. He's got some feeling back in his legs, and the doctors have agreed to start him on physical therapy next week. It will be a hard road, but we're all very hopeful."

"That's *wonderful* news!" Amy exclaimed. She reflected that her own accident with her mother hadn't ended in much hope. But that fact made her root even more fiercely for the Hughes family. She was confident they would pull through.

It would be a few weeks before Kristin's cast came off, Mrs. Hughes said, so she had arranged for Fanfare to stay at Heartland until he was fully at ease with cars and trucks again. Amy was pleased. She had really bonded with the paint horse. And the more time she spent with him, the more convinced she became that she was where she belonged — not buried in books at Virginia Tech, but here at Heartland with the horses and people she loved.

❧

"You shouldn't be doing that, Amy," said Ty later that evening, glancing into the tack room.

Amy was soaping Fanfare's saddle, and she looked up in surprise. "Why not?"

Ty came into the tack room and sat down next to her. "Well, it's just that you're spending all your time around the yard again," he said gently. "Don't you have lots to do for school?"

"Like what?" Amy asked defensively. "Shopping for bedding and new notebooks? I have time."

"I guess," Ty said. "But you got your course list from Virginia Tech, right? I bet you haven't looked at it once."

Amy bit her lip. Leave it to Ty to know exactly that she'd been avoiding anything having to do with college.

"Well, I've *looked* at it," she said eventually. She shrugged uncomfortably. "But I can't get bogged down in that now. I said I'd be here one hundred percent until I go," she said. "Remember?"

Ty nodded, then slipped his arm around her shoulder and gave it a squeeze. Then he got up and left the tack room without a word. Amy rinsed her sponge and reached for the saddle soap again. She hadn't wanted to tell Ty the full truth: She had changed her mind about going to school.

❧

Amy put the tack away and wandered back to the farmhouse, deep in thought. There were no cars in the yard apart from Jack's battered pickup; Ty, Lou, and Joni had all gone home. She went indoors and had a mellow dinner with Grandpa, then left him watching TV and went to her room.

Her course list had fallen off her bedside cabinet and was looking slightly crumpled. She picked it up and scanned it, but it was no use. The words just wouldn't hold her attention. The only things she cared about were Fanfare, Sugarfoot, Spindle, Sundance. Ty and Lou. The new baby. Her family.

She tossed the list aside and lay down, staring at the ceiling. Was there still time to pull out? It had been difficult for everyone on the farm to adjust to the idea of her leaving, but she had been given so much support. And there was Soraya's party, too, that her friend organized especially to say good-bye. And she'd have to let Virginia Tech know.

Amy decided to give herself a few more days to think. Now was not the time to make a snap decision. Whatever she settled on this time would have to be *it* — for good.

Chapter Eleven

For the next two days, the weather was stormy. The wind made all the horses skittish, and several sudden downpours soaked Amy, Ty, and Joni to the skin. Amy was relieved when the sky finally turned calm and bright. Finishing the mucking out early, she went indoors to have breakfast and found Ty standing in the kitchen doorway, chatting with Lou.

Amy took in his crisp, ironed shirt and freshly washed jeans. He was jangling the keys to his pickup in his hands. "Are you going somewhere?" she asked him, sitting down at the table and pouring some coffee.

"Actually, we both are," Ty said, smiling at her. "I'm taking you on a trip."

Amy looked quickly at Lou and Grandpa, her heart beating faster. She didn't want to be paranoid, but it still bothered her that everyone was clearly in on Ty's surprise but her. "What's going on?"

Lou laughed. "Nothing to do with us," she said. "This is all Ty's doing."

Ty smiled and perched himself on a chair. "You might want to put something a little cleaner on," he said, grinning at Amy's grubby yard jeans. "After you've eaten breakfast, of course."

Amy still felt suspicious. "But what about all the work?" she asked, pouring herself a bowl of cereal. "And where are we going?"

"Don't worry about work," said Ty. "Joni's promised to take care of the exercising today. And a day away from the yard will do you good. You'll see where we're going when we get there."

Amy ate her cereal, frustrated but curious. There was no arguing with Ty. She pushed the bowl aside and took a deep breath. "Okay," she said. "I'll get changed."

Ten minutes later, she and Ty climbed into his pickup. Amy was worried that she might react badly to a car ride again, but as he started the engine and turned the vehicle around, she realized that her fear had passed. Join up with Fanfare had brought healing to her as well as to the paint horse. She let out her breath as they drove down the driveway, and Ty glanced at her.

"Are you feeling okay? Tell me if we need to stop for a rest."

She nodded. "I'm fine. I promise."

Ty turned onto the highway, and Amy looked out the window, still feeling bewildered by this mystery trip. Maybe they were just going into town for lunch and to catch a movie, just to give Amy a break. But when they swung onto the freeway, heading away from town, she threw Ty a curious glance. She racked her brains for places he might be taking her — visiting their friend in the Appalachians wouldn't make sense now. It was unlike Ty to whisk her off someplace far without warning. But when she asked him about their destination again, he only shook his head and told her to be patient.

They had been driving for about an hour when suddenly she noticed a sign for Blacksburg. That was where Virginia Tech was located. Amy went cold inside.

"I know where we're going!" she exclaimed. She turned to Ty angrily. "Ty, how *could* you?"

"How could I what?" he asked innocently.

"This is the way to Virginia Tech," said Amy. Her eyes flashed. "You tricked me. You made it sound like it was going to be fun — I thought we were spending a day out together —" She felt close to tears. Ty must have guessed she was having second thoughts about college, so now he was trying to get her excited about it again. Well, his plan wouldn't work!

"It *will* be fun," Ty said quietly. "I thought this would be helpful for you, Amy."

Amy folded her arms and clamped her mouth shut. Inside, she was raging. She couldn't help but feel that Ty was betraying her again. She wished everyone would *stop* deciding what was good for her. Right now, there was no place on earth that she wanted to visit less than Virginia Tech. Not to mention, the school would be closed for the summer. There wouldn't be anything for them to see.

They both remained silent for the last few miles. Then, just as they were turning into the university gates, Ty stared at Amy.

"I wish you'd trust me," he said.

Amy felt choked with anger. She was about to tell Ty to turn right around and drive away when she saw a familiar figure walking toward them. It was Dr. Lovell, a freshman dean and a veterinarian whom she had met at the orientation. He smiled and waved, and Amy realized that it would be rude of her to stay in the pickup. Reluctantly, she stepped out and shook Dr. Lovell's hand. Behind her, Ty started up the pickup again. Amy turned around with her mouth open, but before she could say anything, he was backing up and, with a brief wave, was gone.

"It's good to see you, Amy," said Dr. Lovell, as if he'd been expecting her. "Come on in."

She turned to Dr. Lovell. "I'm not sure why I'm here," she admitted awkwardly.

The dean smiled. "I know," he said. "When Ty called, he explained your situation at Heartland to me. It's not unusual for students to sometimes have their doubts about committing themselves to college for four years. Especially if they feel strongly committed to their life back home. But I think Virginia Tech is the right place for you, Amy. I thought I'd show you a little more of what life will be like here."

Amy's mouth dropped open. Ty had set this up deliberately. She followed Dr. Lovell inside, her anger still bubbling. As if a tour of the campus was going to change anything!

"Of course, you saw all this at orientation," said Dr. Lovell with a smile, gesturing to the campus grounds, which were dotted with impressive modern buildings. "We're only going to my office for my jacket. I'm going to show you something else today. An aspect of the prevet program that you might not have considered before now."

They walked briskly into a building, and along the echoing corridors. Amy glanced into classrooms and laboratories, remembering the buzz at orientation when she had explored the buildings and grounds with other prospective students. It had seemed so exciting then. Now, she felt numb.

They reached the dean's office, and Amy waited outside while he made a brief phone call and picked up his jacket.

"Now," he said as he emerged, "what you won't have

seen before are locations beyond the school, where much of our fieldwork takes place. Of course, you'll have lots of exams and papers in the prevet course of study, but we also give an important role to learning out in the real world."

Amy began to feel curious. "Like . . . on a farm or some-thing?" she asked as they headed to the circular driveway.

"Well, there is a farm and a local stable," said Dr. Lovell. "But Virginia Tech also has connections to other organizations. We try to offer our students as wide a range of experience as possible. There's one place in particular that I'd like you to see."

They climbed into his car, and Amy wondered what sort of establishment they would visit. Dr. Lovell knew all about Heartland; perhaps there was another stable with similar aims close by — though she was sure she'd have heard about it by now if there was. As they drove, Amy still felt bewildered by the surprise of Virginia Tech — and a little upset with Ty — but she was finding her old interest in the school coming alive.

When Dr. Lovell turned off the main road and drove through a magnificent arched gateway, Amy gasped in surprise. They were surrounded by lush greenery. This wasn't like any stable she'd been to before!

"This is Chestnut Hill," Dr. Lovell announced. "It's a girls' boarding school and has top-notch equestrian facilities."

They drove slowly up a smooth drive toward a beautiful white building that looked like an old, colonial-style house. Landscaped grounds stretched out as far as the eye could see, dotted with other old, grand buildings. There was a shiny lake, and a series of pastures on the left. Ponies grazed peacefully beneath the trees, and Amy saw a stable block behind with a large barn and an outdoor schooling ring. It was a lovely, peaceful place, with an air of elegance.

Dr. Lovell steered the car through a gateway next to the stable block and came to a halt. "Come on," he said. "I'll introduce you to the director of riding."

They got out of the car and Amy looked around — up at the beautiful house, and across the green to smaller buildings that looked as though they might be dorms. Everything was immaculate, but the place felt warm and friendly as well; it wasn't hard to imagine the campus swarming with girls, chattering to one another on their way to the stables.

A dark-haired woman dressed in jodhpurs and yard boots came around the corner from the stable block and smiled when she saw them.

"Dr. Lovell! Good to see you," she called.

"Hi, there, Ali," he replied as the young woman came over to meet them. "I'd like you to meet Amy Fleming, one of our prospective students. Amy, this is Ali Carmichael, the new director of riding at Chestnut Hill."

Amy grasped Ali's hand, taking in the warmth of her smile and the clear welcome in her blue eyes.

"Dr. Lovell tells me you're from Heartland, Amy," said Ali. "I've heard a lot about your mother's work. It's so impressive that you've been carrying it on by yourself."

At a loss for words, Amy blushed and gave a modest shrug. She wondered if Ali was waiting for her to say more about her work at Heartland, but to her relief the director of riding seemed eager to tell them about her plans for the new school year instead. They walked companionably toward the stable block, and Ali explained that only two-thirds of the stalls were currently in use.

"They'll fill up at the beginning of term," she said. "Some of the girls bring their own ponies — everyday riding ponies as well as competition horses. They're both equally welcome here. Chestnut Hill has a strong reputation in jumping and equitation. But I see my job as making sure each girl and pony reaches their full potential." Amy nodded, deciding that she liked and trusted Ali.

"This will be Ali's first term here," Dr. Lovell explained. "So I've been letting her know that she has the support of the students and staff at Virginia Tech."

They walked around to the back barn, where the smaller ponies were kept. Amy expected to see a row of classy, well-bred show ponies, but the only things the heads looking over the doors had in common were pricked ears and bright, curious eyes. They were all shapes and sizes — from sturdy beginners' ponies to slender half Thoroughbreds — and all colors, from buckskins to paint horses and bays.

It was such a different environment from Heartland — there had to be at least thirty horses here, and the facilities looked much newer — but Amy felt instantly at home. She imagined groups of girls working together, riding together, and thought how fabulous it would be to have riding available at school, especially if you weren't lucky enough to have horses at home.

"I have lots of plans for the new term," Ali explained. "I want to take a holistic approach to horses, so that the girls will learn stable management as well as riding. Some of our pupils — but not all — come from a privileged background, where they might have staff at home to look after their ponies, so it's even more important that they learn to see their horse as a friend and companion, and not just a way to win ribbons. It will be a very hands-on program."

Instinctively, Amy thought of Green Briar, Heartland's rival, which was owned by Ashley Grant's family. There, horses were often seen as functional, a means to an end, and effort would be put in only if there were guaranteed results. Amy had always suspected that it was an attitude shared by many of the wealthy and privileged — but it seemed that Ali Carmichael thought differently. Her enthusiasm was infectious, and Amy couldn't help thinking that her mom would have loved to meet Ali. Ali's holistic approach to horse owning seemed, in essence, similar to Heartland's philosophy of using alternative therapies alongside conventional medicine. Amy wondered to what extent Ali would try to incorporate holistic methods. It's possible that she'd want some input on problem horses, she thought. Amy was curious about the students. Would they be willing to learn about the different methods of treating horses, from join up to T-touch? She found herself thinking that it would be fun to come and see life at Chestnut Hill once school started.

"Perhaps you'd like to come and talk to the students once the term has started," said Ali, as though she had read Amy's mind. "I'd love them to hear about alternative methods of horse care."

Amy blushed again and smiled. "I'd like that," she said. *If I do go to Virginia Tech, that is,* she thought. But standing here in this yard with these committed, enthusiastic equestrian professionals, she felt suddenly inspired. Heartland would always be her world, but there was so much more she could learn if she was brave enough to expand her horizons. There was a whole *other* world of people who loved horses and were promoting good practices. She could be part of that world, too: That was what Dr. Lovell was trying to show her. And she could give back, in addition to learning; she could take Heartland's teachings — her mother's work — to an even wider audience. And what better place to start than a school?

They wandered around the well-equipped tack and feed rooms, the outdoor training rings, and then the pastures, where Ali pointed out her beautiful dappled gray mare, A Spoonful of Quince.

"Quincy for short," she added, smiling. "I've just turned her out for a few hours, but I'll be training her this afternoon."

"She's gorgeous," Amy whispered. She was dying to ask Ali so many questions: How did she fit training her own horse around her teaching work? Were pupils allowed to ride Quincy? What training methods did she use?

But Amy held back. Now wasn't the time to find out everything about Chestnut Hill. When she returned and there were students around, Amy would really have a chance to explore the experience of attending a school with horses. By the time they walked back to Dr. Lovell's car and said their good-byes, she was smiling.

"Hope to see you in the fall, Amy!" Ali called as she climbed into the passenger seat.

Amy nodded. "I hope so, too," she replied. And, to her surprise, she realized that she meant it.

❧

"Thank you so much for bringing me to Chestnut Hill," Amy said to Dr. Lovell as they drove back to Virginia Tech. "What an amazing place."

The dean smiled. "It is. Has it whetted your appetite for what college will be like?"

Amy hesitated. She knew that from this moment on, there would be no more changing her mind. But she *wanted* to be committed to her future. She was tired of doubting herself, of trying to figure out where she should be headed by always looking backward. At last, Amy was certain about her decision. She took a deep breath and nodded. "Yes," she said. "I can see how much there is to learn. I will be taking my place in the freshman class, Dr. Lovell."

"Good. I'm glad, Amy. I think you'll be a wonderful addition to Virginia Tech." The dean seemed genuinely pleased, and Amy felt touched that he had gone to so much effort to help her make her decision.

But then, as they neared Virginia Tech once more, she realized that it was Ty who had made the greatest effort of all. He was the one who had seen her doubts and contacted Dr. Lovell. Amy's heart was heavy with shame as she thought of how she had resisted and how angry she had been. Ty knew her so well — well enough to recognize when he couldn't persuade her on his own.

Dr. Lovell parked the car and turned to Amy. "Well, I'll look forward to welcoming you in a couple of weeks' time," he said. "And, actually, I'll be teaching one of your classes."

Amy grinned. "I'd better take a closer look at my course list. Thanks again, Dr. Lovell."

As they climbed out of the car, Ty's pickup drove through the gates. Amy hoped he'd forgive her for being so ungracious, and she watched anxiously as he climbed out, stretching his long legs. But she needn't have worried. Ty's face was as open and warm as ever.

"How did it go?" he asked, opening the door for her.

"Oh, Ty." Amy hugged him. "Thank you. I'm sorry I yelled at you. I've really been a handful lately, huh?"

Ty returned her hug, laughing softly. "You're worth the trouble, Amy." As Amy rested her head against his chest, she understood that Ty saw her as much more than someone who shared his life at Heartland. He saw her as her own person. And he knew that she needed to have dreams and ambitions, even ones that reached beyond Heartland.

"I've been checking out the pizza options near here," Ty told her when they finally drew apart. "I figured you'd need to know where the best ones are when you need breaks from cafeteria food. Are you hungry?"

Amy smiled. "Famished." She knew she didn't need to tell Ty that she'd made up her mind about going to college. He knew she'd already found the answer inside herself — he had just taken the trouble to show her the way.

🙟

Amy stared out her bedroom window, playing with the choker around her neck and breathing in the rich scents from Nancy's flower beds. The evening was drawing in. It was almost dark, and moths were beginning to flutter toward her, attracted by the light. She shut the window and took a deep breath.

"Amy! Are you ready?" Nancy's voice came from outside the door. "Ty just got here."

"I'll be down in five minutes!" Amy replied, walking toward her mirror.

The night of Soraya's party had arrived at last. Amy was feeling nervous, and she smoothed her palms carefully down Lou's beautiful blue silk dress. She sprayed perfume on her wrist, reapplied her lip gloss, then looked critically at herself. Her hair didn't look as coiffed as the stylist had made it on graduation day, but Amy preferred the more natural look anyway: half up, with a few wisps around her face. She grabbed her evening bag and slipped on her mules, then opened the door and walked down the stairs.

Ty was waiting for her in the kitchen, his tall, athletic form silhouetted against the window. He turned around as she came in, and his face lit up at the sight of her.

"You look gorgeous." He stepped forward and kissed her gently on the lips. "Are you sure I'm put together enough?"

Amy laughed. Ty looked so handsome in dress slacks and a deep sea-green shirt that accentuated his green eyes. "Don't be silly," she said. "You're perfect." She sighed. "If only I didn't feel like a bundle of nerves."

Ty smiled. "I know. I'm kind of on edge, too. I know it's only Soraya's party, but it feels like more than that somehow."

Their eyes met, and Amy felt a strange mix of emotions — a rush of love for Ty, mingled with sadness. But it *was* more than that. This would be their last night out together for a while. She looked away. She couldn't let herself think about it too much right now.

"I thought you two left already," said Grandpa, coming through from the living room. He stopped when he saw Amy. "Honey, you look beautiful."

"Thank you, Grandpa." Amy offered her cheek for him to kiss. "We're just on our way. Are you sure you don't want to come?"

"Oh, Amy. I'll be in bed just when you two are having your first dance!" He laughed. "Have a wonderful time."

"We will," Ty promised, opening the door for Amy to step out into the cool air. The seemingly endless hot summer days were starting to shorten now, and the nights were crisp with the promise of fall.

They walked to Ty's pickup and Amy slid inside, careful not to snag her silky dress. The drive was only about twenty minutes, and on the way, she began to feel excited at the prospect of seeing all her old classmates, as well as Ben and Daniel and so many others. But to her surprise, Ty turned down a little side road half a mile from Soraya's.

"What's this? A shortcut?" Amy asked curiously. "I

don't think I've been down here before." She peered out into the darkness, but all she could see was trees.

Ty didn't answer but drove into a parking spot and turned off the engine. Amy looked at him expectantly, her pulse suddenly racing. What was going on?

"Ty?" she queried.

He was fumbling in the breast pocket of his jacket. He fished something out and turned to Amy, his expression serious but slightly anxious.

"There's just something I'd like to say, before we go into the party," he said. "And . . . something I'd like to give you."

"*Give* me?" Amy felt breathless. She studied Ty's face, lit up in the moonlight.

He reached for her right hand. "I wanted you to know that whatever happens after this summer, I'm here for you, Amy." His eyes met hers, searching. "I hope you know that."

She nodded. "I've always known that. But when you took me to Virginia Tech, I realized just how fully you support me. You helped me realize that going to college isn't about leaving Heartland, it's about discovering new places. And eventually bringing my mom's work to even more people."

Ty smiled, his green eyes bright. "There's a big old world out there," he agreed quietly. "And a whole lot of horses. But wherever you are, whatever you're doing, I hope you'll think of me."

Amy gasped as Ty held a glinting ring out to her. She looked down. It was exquisite — a silver ring with a tiny pair of hands holding a heart in its center. The heart was topped by a small crown.

"It's a claddagh ring," Ty explained, running the tip of his finger over the metal. "It's an old Irish symbol of friendship . . . and love. If your heart is free, you wear the heart facing outward. But if your heart belongs to someone, you wear it facing in."

Her heart fluttering, Amy slid the delicate ring onto her finger, making sure the heart faced inward.

"Just something to remember me by," Ty added.

Amy felt tears welling up — tears of happiness and sorrow all mixed in together. She swallowed hard and brushed them away, staring at the ring on her finger and then up at Ty's loving face. She leaned across the seat and threw her arms around his neck, burying her face in his jacket.

"Oh, Ty," she whispered. "I don't need something to remember you by. I'll always be thinking of you. Every minute." She felt as though she never wanted to move from that spot, with Ty holding her, his fingers stroking her neck. But she pulled back and smiled, staring deep into his gentle green eyes.

"But I love it," she whispered, wiping the tears from her cheeks. "This is the most beautiful thing anyone has ever given me." She took a deep breath. "And I'll always wear it, no matter what. My heart will always belong to you."

Chapter Twelve

Amy felt gloriously light-headed as she and Ty stepped through Soraya's front door. It felt surreal to be going from such a private moment straight into the hubbub of a party, but at the same time it was exhilarating. She squeezed Ty's hand, looking around. The front room had been completely cleared to make room for everyone, and the whole house was festooned in ribbons and fairy lights. The party was just beginning to pick up, with lots of people arriving. As Soraya's father ushered them into the living room, Amy spotted Ben and Tara talking to Joni.

Soraya rushed across the room to greet them. She looked stunning in a purple dress that set off her dark curls to perfection.

"You made it! I was scared you might decide against

this party, too," she joked. "Come and get a drink. We've been mixing fruit punch all afternoon."

Amy grinned at Ty as they followed Soraya to the kitchen. Her friend was already beginning to look every inch the stage actress, graceful and confident, with the power to command everyone's attention.

Matt was pouring drinks and joking that Soraya was going to keep him in the kitchen all evening. "She's got me trained," he was saying to someone as he handed out glasses. He grinned and waved as Amy and Ty made their way over with Soraya.

"What were you saying about me?" demanded Soraya.

"Nothing, nothing at all," said Matt, smiling at Amy. She accepted a glass of punch and took a sip. For all Matt's joking about Soraya's hold on him, it was clear that their choices for college would take them in pretty different directions. As Amy watched her two friends bantering together, it seemed that they were relaxed and open to whatever the future might bring. Amy looked down at the new ring on her finger, utterly secure in her future with Ty.

She followed Ty back into the main room, where Lou and Scott had just arrived. They gathered in a circle with Joni, Daniel, Ben, and Tara and joined the energetic conversation. Everybody pestered Lou to reveal the names she and Scott had been discussing for the baby — Jack for a boy, and Georgia Marion if it was a girl.

Music started up in one corner and people began to dance. Amy and Ty watched other couples circle on the dance floor. Matt led Soraya into the center, and Ben soon followed with Tara.

"Shall we?" Ty asked, smiling at Amy when the music changed.

Amy nodded. They found a space and began to dance, with Ty's hand resting lightly in the small of her back. It felt wonderful to be so close, in their own little world, as if the people around them weren't there. But as the song came to an end, she saw Ben standing on his own while Tara chatted with Joni. She gave Ty a kiss on the cheek, and she went over to say hello.

"I heard about your accident," Ben said, once they had exchanged greetings. "You look fine now. Are you OK?"

Amy nodded. "It was just a mild concussion," she explained. "We still have Fanfare at Heartland, though I'm hoping he'll be ready to leave by the time I do."

Ben looked at her thoughtfully. "Heartland won't be the same without you, Amy," he said. "How's everyone going to cope?"

Amy ran her finger around the rim of her glass. "I've been obsessing over that for the last few weeks," she admitted. "Heartland isn't the same without you, either, you know. But you're doing so well at Nick's. And Joni's terrific. I guess the thing is, people come and go, but as Ty said, Heartland will always be there."

"You're right," Ben said thoughtfully. "That's a smart way to think about it."

Amy smiled and glanced at the dance floor. To her surprise, she saw Daniel dancing with Ashley Grant, laughing and chatting away.

Ben followed her gaze and raised an eyebrow. "Now there's an unlikely duo," he commented.

It was true. Daniel had worked for a while at Green Briar but had left as soon as he could to move to Nick Halliwell's. Green Briar was dominated by Valerie Grant, Ashley's mother, who had very rigid ideas about how to train horses. Daniel was much happier now, working with high-quality competition horses such as Amy's old horse, Storm.

But as Amy watched Ashley flick her long blond hair over her shoulder, she shrugged. "Well, I guess they have things in common," she pointed out. "Ashley's not going away to college. She's going to help her mom run Green Briar. I guess it makes sense for her to keep up with people at other stables."

Ben nodded. "I know Ashley's difficult, but I get the sense that she's not as stern as her mother," he said. "Maybe she'll be good for Green Briar in the long run. You never know."

"That would be something." Amy grinned, and they laughed as Matt walked up to join them.

Matt bowed in front of Amy and then offered her his arm. "Will you do me the honor of dancing, Miss Fleming?" he asked. "Do excuse us, Ben."

Ben grinned and stepped back as Tara returned to his side. "Of course."

Amy followed Matt onto the dance floor. He looked very handsome in a dark blue shirt and pressed tan trousers, and Amy could easily picture him striding around hospital wards in a long white coat.

"So it's actually happening," she said as they began to dance. "We graduated from high school. We're all going our separate ways."

"I know," said Matt, looking around at the throng. "But this isn't the end, Amy. We'll all come back eventually. Right?"

Amy looked at him. Of course it was true — there were still the vacations, and she fully expected to return to Heartland once she had finished with all her schooling. But Matt? Somehow, she didn't think he'd be a local from now on. "Will you?" she asked gently.

Matt's gaze rested on Soraya, who was dancing with Jason, one of Matt's friends from school. "Well . . . I guess I don't really know," he admitted. "There's so much I love here. And our new niece or nephew to look forward to!"

"I can't wait," Amy enthused.

Matt nodded, and then studied her. "But I don't know where life will take me. I'm not sure if I'll end up back here. But I'm sure you will."

Amy glanced over at Ty, who was talking to Matt's brother, Scott. "That's my plan. But four years is a long time. And I'll be going to vet school, too."

Matt spun her around, making her laugh. His brown eyes smiled at her, and he, too, glanced across at Ty. "You know what I think?" he said.

Amy shook her head.

"Some things are just bigger than time," said Matt. "And they're the things that are well worth waiting for."

❧

As Amy lay in bed that night, images of the party flitted through her head — snatches of conversation, the whirling colors of people's dresses, and the smiling faces of all her friends. No one had noticed the ring on her finger. Feeling slightly self-conscious, she had kept it out of sight for most of the evening. But now she played with it, looking at the delicate engraving in the faint moonlight that came in from the window. Content, she drifted into sleep, and when she woke there was sunlight streaming into the room. She could hear the faint sound of voices in the kitchen. She realized she must have overslept. Quickly, she threw on some clothes and bounded downstairs.

"Hello, sleeping beauty," Grandpa greeted her with a grin.

Amy rubbed her eyes and sat down at the kitchen table. "What time is it?" she asked. Lou was already there, opening the mail, and Nancy was at the stove making coffee.

"Just before ten," Grandpa informed her.

Amy stared at him. "Ten!" Since she'd recovered from the fall, she'd gone back to her habit of rising at dawn. Sleeping in felt like a rare luxury.

"Well, as I recollect, you didn't get in until two o'clock last night," he said. "I think you're allowed to sleep in."

Lou smiled at her. "We left a lot earlier than you and Ty," she said. "I was feeling pretty tired. But the party was still in full swing." Her eyes drifted to Amy's right hand, and Amy moved it quickly off the table. So someone *had* noticed — Lou!

"Ty and Joni haven't been here long," added Grandpa. "I thought we'd wait for you, then call them in for breakfast. How about scrambled eggs and bacon?"

"Sounds delicious," agreed Amy. She caught Lou's eye and smiled. She knew she wouldn't be able to escape a grilling from her sister about the ring.

Grandpa and Nancy got to work while Amy and Lou set the table, then Amy went outside to find Ty and Joni. They both looked tired after their own late nights, but they perked up when Amy invited them in for breakfast. As they walked up to the farmhouse, Joni told Amy and

Ty how Jasmine and Sundance had been playing together in the pasture earlier.

"I don't know what was wrong with them," she laughed. "They were chasing each other around the field as if they'd both been stung by a bee."

Ty and Amy exchanged glances. "Old friends," said Amy knowingly. "I don't suppose it was Sundance doing the chasing, was it?"

"Now that you mention it . . ." Joni said.

"Thought so," said Amy with a grin. "Up to his old tricks. Joni, you have to make sure you don't let him get away with too much mischief while I'm not here!"

They went inside. The smell of sizzling bacon filled the kitchen, and Amy realized she was starving. Platefuls of breakfast were demolished in no time as everyone dug in, all talking at once about Soraya's party. Joni had witnessed Daniel exchanging phone numbers with a striking redhead, while Lou had had a long conversation with a cousin of Soraya's about the trials of pregnancy. Luckily, Lou herself had little to no morning sickness, and, Amy thought, she looked more serene than ever.

When she could eat no more, Amy pushed her plate aside with a happy sigh. She was grateful to Soraya for organizing the party and decided to call her later to thank her and compare notes. The party had brought so many people together and had somehow given Amy a sense of peace. She fiddled with her claddagh ring and smiled to herself. Even though she hadn't said a separate good-bye to everyone there, she still felt as if the party had offered a wonderful sense of closure.

❧

Later that morning, Amy was clearing empty feed sacks out of the feed room when Grandpa popped his head around the door.

"Ah! There you are," he said.

Amy looked at him expectantly. "Did you want me for something?"

"When you're finished," said Grandpa. "There's no rush. Come and find me in the garden."

"I will." Mystified, Amy folded the empty sacks and swept up the bits of spilled grain, then went around the side of the yard to the garden. Grandpa was standing at the far gate, where the garden had a view of the driveway and the smallest Heartland field. In the middle of the pasture was a young oak tree marking the last resting place of Pegasus, the talented gray show jumper that had belonged to Marion.

"Grandpa?" Amy touched him on the arm.

He turned, and Amy saw that his eyes were misty. "Amy." He smiled. "Let's go for a walk, sweetie."

He opened the gate into the pasture, and they wandered

toward the oak tree. It had grown a good deal in the last eighteen months or so. It was no longer a sapling, and birds already enjoyed the shade of its branches.

"I know I've said this before," said Grandpa. "But I just wanted to tell you how proud I am of what you've achieved, Amy. We'll all miss you so much, but Marion would have wanted you to do everything that was within your reach. You know that, don't you?"

Amy nodded. "Yes, Grandpa. I do know that now."

Jack Bartlett drew an envelope from his back pocket. "And this is something to help you along your path," he said. "Your life is going to change in so many different ways. It won't always be easy, and sometimes the unexpected may knock you sideways. So I've kept this money aside for when you might need it. Keep it safe."

Amy stared down at the envelope in her hands. "Grandpa! I can't accept this . . ."

"Of course you can," he said firmly. He reached over and hugged her. "What's mine is already yours and Lou's, Amy. Heartland, the farm — everything. This is just to provide some extra help."

Amy felt her throat grow tight and she stared at her grandfather. Her eyes traveled over his gray hair and the crow's-feet that defined his smiling eyes. "Thank you, Grandpa," she managed to whisper.

"You and Lou mean the world to me," he said. "And I

wish you both the greatest happiness that life can give. I can't think of any two people who deserve it more."

❧

Amy went upstairs with the envelope and put it safely in a drawer. She felt choked up, and she sat on the bed for a moment, gathering her thoughts. The realities of leaving were sinking in. She looked up at her suitcase, stacked on top of her wardrobe, and began to think of what she would have to take with her — books, clothes, her stereo. And she should probably ask Lou to take her shopping. Then she stopped herself. *Not yet.* She still wanted to soak up every last minute of home. She stood and went downstairs.

When she stepped outside, a surprising sight met her eyes. Lou was leading Sugarfoot across the yard, encouraging the little pony to take quicker, more confident steps. "Come on. You can do it," Amy heard her say.

Amy watched closely. There was still a wobble in the Shetland's hind legs, but he was steadier than he had been in weeks. And in the bright sunlight, she could see that his haunches were beginning to flesh out again, too.

Lou looked up and saw Amy standing there. "Isn't he doing great?" she exclaimed. "He's really started to pick up in the last week or so. Scott thinks he's definitely going to pull through, and he means it."

Amy felt happiness fizz through her. "Wow! He looks like a brand-new pony!"

"Hear that, Sugarfoot?" Lou stopped and allowed him to rest, while Amy scratched his neck and withers.

Sugarfoot snorted and shook his mane, then nudged at Amy for treats in his familiar impish way.

"I don't have anything, honey." She laughed. "You're going to have to wait till Lou gets you back in your stall."

Lou turned the pony around and gently urged him forward. Sugarfoot began to walk again, his steps tottering. "He still gets tired quickly," said Lou. "And it's going to take a while to regain the strength in his muscles. But we're getting there, aren't we, boy?" She smiled happily. "Scott says your idea might have made all the difference, Amy. He says we've given him the strength to fight, which is half the battle with a lot of illnesses."

Amy grinned. She was relieved for Lou — and the Shetland. And she felt particularly pleased that she had helped with his recovery in some way. This was exactly what she wanted to offer in her future career: an approach that offered healing in whatever way it was needed, not necessarily constrained by science or conventional medications. She turned away to go down to the back barn feeling confident about the path that lay ahead, however distant it seemed right now.

She decided to work with Fanfare. The paint horse seemed almost completely recovered, but there was one thing that Amy hadn't yet tried, and she wanted Ty's support before she attempted it.

Ty was lunging Mischief and raised his whip in greeting when he saw Amy. "I'm almost done here!" he called.

Amy sat on the gate to wait. Mischief was looking good. His hocks were tucked right under him as he trotted around Ty, driving powerfully forward with long, springy strides. Ty brought him back to an active walk, and then to a halt.

"Good boy," Ty praised him, gathering in the lunge line as Amy jumped off the gate. He turned to Amy. "Is everything OK?"

Amy smiled and nodded. "I just saw Lou with Sugarfoot. He's so much better. He's going to be all right, Ty."

"That's terrific!" Ty looked relieved. "He *has* been looking brighter for a few days now. Your idea for treatment sure paid off."

They walked to the gate, and Amy broached the subject of Fanfare. "I think it's time we took him out on the roads," she said. "Not the route I took when we fell, but maybe a short stretch on the way up the ridge. What do you think?"

Ty looked pensive. "Well, that's definitely ground we need to cover before he goes home," he agreed. "But I don't want you to go alone. I'll come with you."

"I was hoping you'd say that," said Amy. "Who do you want to ride?"

"Attitude's going home tomorrow," he said. "It would be nice to take him out for one last ride."

"Great," Amy said determinedly. This wasn't just about Fanfare facing his last fears — by taking him out on the road, she'd be facing her own.

She got Fanfare's tack and went to the back barn. Then, once Ty had caught Attitude and saddled him up, they told Joni where they were going and set out along the track. Fanfare was alert and eager to get onto the trail, twitching his ears at different sounds in the woods, his stride brisk and confident. Amy and Ty pushed the horses into a trot, and by the time they reached the track that led on to one of the local lanes, both were nicely warmed up.

"Down here?" Amy suggested. "We can just do half a mile on the road, then come back to the trail."

"Should be fine," agreed Ty. "I'll lead the way, OK?"

They walked sedately down to the road and turned onto it in single file. Fanfare tensed up as soon as his hooves clopped onto the paved surface, but Amy kept a steady contact with her legs and reins to reassure him. With Attitude up ahead, the paint horse was already doing much better than he had when they'd been out alone.

She heard the sound of a car engine and shortened her

reins, reassuring herself that they would be fine. She whispered soothing sounds in Fanfare's pricked-up ear.

Ty glanced back. "A car's coming. How's he doing?"

Amy nodded. "He's fine. A bit nervous, that's all."

"And you?" said Ty, looking at her carefully.

Amy smiled. "I'm fine, too." She had to trust Fanfare just as much as she was asking him to have faith in her. Riding horses was all about partnership. The fact that they had both been scared together that time had to be a source of strength more than anything else.

The car approached slowly, and Amy kept up a gentle pressure with her legs, murmuring to the gelding to keep him calm. Fanfare balked, jogging on the spot, but Amy kept her eyes fixed on Ty and drove Fanfare forward, never allowing him to forget that she was there. Her heart in her throat, she prayed that the bond of trust formed by join up would not be broken now. Fanfare needed to draw courage from her — and for his sake, she needed to find it.

The car passed by, and Amy let out a sigh of relief. "Good boy. Well done." She breathed, relaxing her pressure on the reins. "That wasn't so bad, was it?"

Fanfare snorted, and Amy realized how relieved he must have felt as well. The burden of fear was a heavy one to carry, and it was wonderful to see the signs of it lifting. Fanfare was well on the way to a happier future. Around her, the road was lit up with sunlight, and the birds were filling the air with their song. Any sense of dread lifted.

Amy would never forget what had happened to her and her mother, but the trauma no longer haunted her. There was too much lightness in life to let the darkness overwhelm you, Amy reflected.

Ty turned off the road and climbed back up toward Clairdale Ridge. Where the track widened out, they gave the horses their head and laughed out loud as Attitude and Fanfare set off at a fast canter, side by side.

At the top of the ridge they stopped and turned the horses' faces to the breeze. Amy was still exhilarated from the canter and leaned down to pat Fanfare's neck happily. Her claddagh ring glinted in the sunlight, and she looked up to smile at Ty. She was reminded of the ride they had shared at the start of the summer.

"It's moments like this when I wonder how I can ever leave this place," she mused aloud.

Ty smiled. "Don't worry. You'll keep Heartland with you, even when you're away."

"You're right," Amy said. "Absence doesn't always mean forgetting. I think I've finally learned that. I mean, my mom has been gone for so long now, but . . ." She shook her head. "She still lives on in so many ways."

"She lives on in you," Ty said, reaching over to caress Amy's cheek. "You and Lou."

And Lou's baby, Amy realized. In less than a year, there

would be new life at Heartland. Amy wondered if her future niece or nephew would inherit Marion's love for and devotion to horses. Amy couldn't imagine it any other way.

"Yes," Amy said, taking Ty's hand. "But her spirit is especially alive in the work we do. And while I'm away, I know I can trust you to keep doing her work. I know it's hard, but I also know how much you love it."

"It's an honor, actually." Ty squeezed Amy's hand.

They smiled at each other, promising more with their eyes than they ever could with words. This was the meaning of trust, Amy thought. Knowing that someone was by your side no matter what — helping you fight your battles and achieve your goals, and always having faith in you, even when you lost sight of your own strengths.

Then, without another word, they turned their horses toward the bright sun and cantered along the ridge, the sound of hoofbeats echoing through the trees in harmony with the wind and the birdsong.

Here is a sneak preview of Lauren Brooke's new series

Chestnut Hill

THE NEW CLASS

"Dylan, we're almost there. Wake up, honey."

Dylan Walsh heard the words and blinked her eyes open. Glancing out the window, she saw whitewashed fences lining lush green pastures. "What?" Dylan murmured. "Why'd you guys let me go to sleep?"

"We just got off the interstate a few minutes ago," her dad explained.

Dylan's mom looked over her shoulder into the back-seat of the family SUV. "You'd didn't miss anything. I thought you probably needed the rest."

Dylan made a point of pouting before brushing her red hair behind her ears and turning her gaze back out the window. Dylan didn't want to admit that her mom was right. She had not been able to sleep a wink the night before. There had been too many things going through her head. She'd been looking forward to this day for so long — she was really on her way to Chestnut Hill! She searched the fields for any signs of horses, trying to gauge how close they were to the school. She wondered if all of Virginia was this picturesque.

Dylan followed the stretch of fence toward the horizon and her heart pounded when she saw the brick pillars that marked the entrance of the esteemed boarding school.

"This is it!" she yelled, recalling the first time she had visited the school. After the prospective-student weekend that spring, Dylan had been set on coming to Chestnut Hill.

She rolled down the window to get a better glimpse of the iron gates at the start of the drive. As her dad turned the car, Dylan's eyes focused on the Chestnut Hill crest. The chestnut tree (*what else*? she thought delightedly) with spreading roots and branches was worked into the ornate iron gate along with the profile of a horse's head.

The white rail fences continued on either side of the

driveway, and Dylan shielded her eyes from the sun to scan the paddocks for the Chestnut Hill horses. She thought they were all beautiful, but she held her breath as she searched for one pony in particular.

Before Dylan could find the familiar brown-and-white coat, the car turned to follow the gravel drive and the rest of the grounds came into view. Dylan leaned forward as they approached the Old House, the magnificent white colonial building that had been the original school, more than one hundred years ago. Dylan recognized the regal structure from all of the school's brochures. With its tall white pillars, it gave Chestnut Hill a look of great southern tradition. Now the Old House just held faculty and administration offices, and the classrooms and science labs were in classic redbrick buildings on the other side of the campus. Ever since the fourth grade, when she read about it in *Horse and Rider* magazine, Dylan had wanted to go to Chestnut Hill because of its top-tier riding program. *I can't believe I'm actually here*, she thought, with a slight shiver of excitement.

From the moment she had laid eyes on the campus that spring, she had been imagining this moment. Everything about the school was the best that money could buy: the Olympic-size swimming pool, the indoor track, the art studio complete with ceramics workshop and kiln. And the school was well known for high academic standards that prepared students for acceptance into the most competitive colleges, which was enough to please her parents.

Mr. Walsh took a left turn, following the signs to the dorms on the north side of the campus. There were six houses where students slept, studied, and generally hung out. Dylan already knew that she was in Adams House, which, very conveniently, was the dorm closest to the stable yard. She slid across the leather seat so she could look out of the other window, and tapped a drum-roll with her fingers as they passed the stables. *I'm going to be able to walk to the barn in less than five minutes*, she thought. *I'll be the most dedicated rider at Chestnut Hill. Just wait until team tryouts!*